KISS THE BLOOD OFF MY HANDS

GERALD BUTLER

Introduction by Curtis Evans

STARK HOUSE

Stark House Press • Eureka California

KISS THE BLOOD OFF MY HANDS

Published by Stark House Press
1315 H Street
Eureka, CA 95501, USA
griffinskye3@sbcglobal.net
www.starkhousepress.com

KISS THE BLOOD OFF MY HANDS
Originally published by Nicholson & Watson, London, 1940; reprinted by
Jarrolds Publishing, London, 1940; and Farrar & Rinehart, Inc. New York,
1946, copyright © 1946 by Gerald Butler. Reprinted in paperback by Dell
Books, New York, 1948, as *The Unafraid*.

Reprinted by permission of the agent on behalf of the Gerald Butler
estate. All rights reserved under International and Pan-American
Copyright Conventions.

"What Bloody Man Wrote That?" © 2024 by Curtis Evans

ISBN: 979-8-88601-088-6

Cover & Text design by Mark Shepard, shepgraphics.com
Proofreading by Bill Kelly

First Stark House Press Edition: June 2024

KISS THE BLOOD OFF MY HANDS

Bill is just off the boat in England and already he's killed someone. The bouncer had it coming, but still, Bill knows he's got to lay low until the hunt cools off. He's too canny to keep running—he picks an unlocked flat and helps himself to a temporary hideout. Which is how he meets Jane—it's her flat.

She lets him stay the night, but that's it. Bill doesn't tell her about the dead bouncer and moves on, but he can't forget Jane's face. There's just something about her. So he finds out where she's works, and starts asking her out. How could either of them know that such an unlikely meeting could lead to love… and another murder?

> "It's punch and pace will stun you."
> —James Hadley Chase

Gerald Butler Bibliography
(1907-1988)

Novels:
Kiss the Blood Off My Hands (1940; reprinted in U.S.
  as *The Unafraid*, 1948)
They Cracked Her Glass Slipper (1941)
Their Rainbow Had Black Edges (1943; reprinted in U.S.
  as *Dark Rainbow*, 1945)
Mad With Much Heart (1945; reprinted in U.S.
  as *The Lurking Man*, 1952)
Slippery Hitch (1946)
Blow Hot, Blow Cold (1951; reprinted in U.S.
  as *Choice of Two Women*, 1960)
There Is a Death, Elizabeth (1972)

What Bloody Man Wrote That?
Gerald Butler's *Kiss the Blood off My Hands* (1940)

by Curtis Evans

British crime fiction of the Twenties and Thirties—the so-called Golden Age of detective fiction—remains most strongly associated with the classic clue-puzzle tradition of Agatha Christie and her colleagues and all the trimmings which this tradition so often entailed: eccentric Great Detectives, fiendishly clever criminals, country houses, stately butlers, adenoidal maids, quaint villages, absent-minded vicars, deaths in locked rooms, bodies in libraries, bizarre murder methods, dramatic revelations before assembled suspects in the final chapter and, last but not least, finical avoidance of the depiction of explicit sex and violence—though sadly the latter all too human pastimes typically are prime components of murders as they are actually carried out in real life. It was Anglo-American hard-boiled crime writer Raymond Chandler in his 1944 essay "The Simple Art of Murder" who famously credited his predecessor Dashiell Hammett (along with other, lesser-known American pulp writers of the Twenties and Thirties) with taking "murder out of the Venetian vase and dropping it into the alley," thereby giving it "back to the kind of people who commit it for reasons, not just to provide a corpse; and with the means at hand, not with hand-wrought dueling pistols, curare, and tropical fish." In the 1930s the American reading public eagerly devoured new school American crime fiction as it made its way into novel form, yet British readers—and particularly the newsprint influencers who reviewed and wrote about crime fiction—were slower to embrace Hammett and other tough guy upstarts.

While American reviewers lauded Hammett novels like *Red Harvest* (1929) and *The Maltese Falcon* (1930) as something startlingly new and bracing in crime fiction, their British contemporaries often could not help but shudder with displeasure at the author's brutal touch. "This is a typical example of American crime fiction," prissily observed the anonymous "Literary Reviewer" in the Liverpool *Evening Standard* of Hammett's *The Maltese Falcon*, "but the continual use of blasphemous epithets somewhat mars a good story." In his *Masters of Mystery: A Study of the Detective Story* (1931), British scholar H. Douglas Thomson observed tersely and decidedly unenthusiastically of Hammett's private eye Sam Spade that he "is an honest-to-goodness, 100 percent American detective. There does not appear to be much more than this to commend him."

But despite squeamish reviewers who turned up their noses at violent American crime writing about vicious gangsters and police "third degree," Dashiell Hammett and his tough school was not to be denied, even across the pond in that cozy never-never land of tea and crumpets, as Anglophile mystery readers liked to imagine it. In the second half of the 1930s mainstream English novelist Graham Greene published his highly-regarded seamy murder thriller *Brighton Rock* (1938), while two neophyte English crime writers, Peter Cheyney and James Hadley Chase, took the tough route with their work. (Their real life, posh-sounding monikers were Reginald Evelyn Peter Southouse-Cheyney and Rene Lodge Brabazon Raymond.)

Cheyney, a Metropolitan Police reporter and crime investigator and a onetime member of Oswald Mosley's New Party (a precursor to the later British Union of Fascists), launched two hard-fisted detective series in 1936 and 1938, which were respectively headlined by an FBI agent improbably named Lemmy Caution and a British private detective named Slim Callaghan. Cheyney quickly became one of the United Kingdom's most popular crime writers in 1944, for example, racking up sales of more than 1.5 million copies of his books internationally. When in 1951 the high-living author passed away at the age of fifty-five, he left an estate worth, in modern value, some two million pounds, or about 2.5 million dollars—proving that crime very much did pay for some writers.

Meanwhile, in 1939 Chase published *No Orchids for Miss Blandish*, a shameless rip-off of American author William Faulkner's seamy, controversial self-styled crime "potboiler" *Sanctuary* (1931). *Orchids* became a smash success, sweeping in its wake even squeamish British reviewers. To be sure, some of them held the traditional stolid British line. Frank Swinnerton in the London *Observer* briefly dismissed *Orchids* as a "coarse shocker about kidnapping gangsters" (one can almost see him holding his nose), while another reviewer sniffed: "It is just like an American gangster film with the inclusion of several things which the gangster films have the decency to leave out. If there are people who really like gangster films, they may like this book." However, other tastemakers were much more positive, seemingly almost in spite of themselves. "It is doubtful if the vile ruthlessness of gangsterdom has ever been more vividly presented in fiction," allowed one, while another gasped: "It made me have palpitations and go wan in the cheeks."

The public sided with those who came to praise, rather than to bury, the author. *Orchids* sold over half a million copies in the next five years and launched Chase on the course of a highly prolific and profitable crime writing career that on more than one occasion included outright plagiarism of American authors. Raymond Chandler's British publisher, Hamish Hamilton, extracted a public apology from Chase for his, erm, borrowings from Chandler's *The Big Sleep* (1939) in his novel *Blondes' Requiem* (1945). (I found that it plagiarizes Hammett's *Red Harvest* as well.) However, Chase's career was not in the least checked by this embarrassment—indeed, quite the opposite. So, if one simply must steal, steal from the best!

With the successful examples of Cheney and Chase before them, additional aspiring British novelists decided that, despite their native country's genteel reputation, a significant segment of its citizenry evidently liked their reading rough. One of these acutely perceptive aspirants was thirty-four-year-old Englishman Gerald Butler, who in 1939, when he wrote his first novel, was then an executive in the big London advertising firm of Pritchard, Wood and Partners. In his autobiography *Here Lies*, espionage writer Eric Ambler, who like Butler (and detective novelist Dorothy L. Sayers) worked in advertising between the wars, recalled: "Most [advertising] copywriters wished that they could be writing something else.... Gerald Butler...did well...with a novel called *Kiss the Blood off My Hands*." Indeed, he did.

When Gerald Butler published *Kiss the Blood off My Hands*—a violent saga of murder and other assorted acts of mayhem with a murderous lout as its protagonist—in England in 1940 the novel came complete with a laudatory blurb from none other than James Hadley Chase, who pithily avowed of it: "Its punch and pace will stun you." Yet many critics cold-shouldered Butler's book, despite the relatively warm reception they had afforded *Orchids*. It seems that Butler had erred, as far as they were concerned, in making a "hero" out of a brutish killer. (Chase's bad 'uns at least were clearly delineated as bad 'uns.) Observed one reviewer briefly and backhandedly: "If you can work up any sympathy for a ham-fisted bully, you will revel in this story of a thug." Another, Harold M.

Dowling of the Cardiff *Western Mail*, penned a lengthier pan, in which he condemned as well the recent phenomenon of British writers aping their earthier American cousins:

> Mr. Butler's new book is one of those tough stories which some of the modern American writers do impressively. Somehow or other, however, it fails to impress when manufactured with English materials and placed in an English setting, and the sense of incongruity one gets from this story is perhaps an apt commentary on the difference of social atmosphere in the two countries. The hero (hero?) is tough enough, to be sure. A great, ruthless bully, he smashes the life out of a man in a public-house and then takes refuge in a young girl's bedroom. Thenceforward, he drags the girl, fearfully fascinated, with him on a career of theft and brutal violence…. An interesting enough novel to read, but you can't make a hero out of a ruffian.

Yet in spite of newspaper naysayers *Blood* made a big hit with British readers and was reprinted the same year by the publisher Jarrolds, who claimed that during World War Two they sold almost a quarter of a million copies of the novel in England alone. Despite this success, *Blood* finally made it to the United States, so the story goes, on the strength of what American book reviewer and onetime mystery writer Nancy Barr Mavity, dubbed a "freak of undesigned publicity." It seems that in 1942 an American sailor came across a battered, coverless copy of *Blood* on a transport in Samoa and began reading it aloud to some of his buddies who were lolling on the gun deck. Impressed with what they heard, the men dissected this real "he-man" book into chapters and passed them around, only to be dismayed when they found that the last two chapters were missing. In New Zealand the sailors scoured bookstores for a copy of *Blood*, but to no avail. After the transport was sunk in the 1943 Solomon Islands campaign, survivor Lloyd Powers, one of those enraptured readers from the gun deck, made it back in January 1944 to San Diego Naval Hospital, where during his convalescence he begged help in finding a copy of *Blood* from forty-three-year-old county librarian Jeanette Barry, the widow of a lately deceased San Diego cop, but again to no avail, even after she in turn sought assistance from *Publishers Weekly*.

Time magazine recounted these events as a human-interest story later that year, with the result that the novel was picked up by American publisher Farrar and Rinehart in 1945, along with a pair of novels that Butler had published in England since *Blood*: *Their Rainbow Had Black Edges* (1943; as *Dark Rainbow*) and *Mad with Much Heart* (1945). When *Blood* appeared for the first time in the United States in April 1946, it scored with critics, who compared Gerald Butler to author James M. Cain of *The Postman Always Rings Twice* notoriety. "[A] high powered novel," enthused Ralph M. Williams of the *Chicago Tribune*, "sustains suspense to the last page." In the *Nashville Banner* Louise Douglas Morrison allowed of *Blood* that some readers would like it and some hate it, but declared that she herself thought highly of its "well-constructed plot heightened by excellently handled suspense and realistically drawn characters." Ray Gould of the *Montgomery Advertiser* raved that "devotees of the James M. Cain-Raymond Chandler school of reading will revel in the high-tension explosiveness of this blistering melodrama.... For sheer uninhibited, high-powered emotional impact it would be hard to find a novel to equal it.... the furious pace will keep you reading wide-eyed and breathless until the very last page."

An especially thoughtful take on the novel came from the hand of another Alabamian: Lee McBride White, a thirty-one-year-old reviewer at the *Birmingham News* and a past *Weird Tales* devotee and youthful correspondent with horror writer H. P. Lovecraft. "This is a story of pure violence," he declared, expounding:

> Without keeping anything like an accurate score of events, it is possible to remember three or four murders, a case of attempted rape, a brutal flogging, blackmail, and numberless casual robberies, beatings and assorted crimes.... There is enormous suspense. As the protagonist (who is writing his own story in a style as simple and direct as a belch) makes the rounds of his grim, cheap and hopeless life, a rather preposterous sympathy grows within the mind of the reader. Where do people like Bill Saunders come from? What has gone wrong with the world, that it produces such people?... We get no apologies and no explanations from this author. He has no creed, no qualms and no compunction. Censors who chew their fingernails to the quick worrying about how much of a thigh is showing in some particular movie had better take off their dunce caps and begin to worry about a world in which such men as Butler's hero live, where vice is its own reward, where people meet only to clash, where there is always a victim and always a victor, where compromise is something out of another world.

Kiss the Blood off My Hands is a sociological document, if you want to take it seriously. If you don't want to take it seriously, it is as ripe and gaudy a tale of crime and action as you will find in the English language. Either way, you will read it to the end, not only without stopping, but probably without stopping at the ends of sentences. The action runs together like poured molasses, and the reader will find himself stuck fast in it.

Even in the U.S. some reviewers were appalled by the book, however. In the *Wisconsin State Journal* Harry Hansen worried at the moral implications for the world were such works of fiction to capture the imaginations of the public:

Heaven help us if we get any more stories like *Kiss the Blood off My Hands* or if the motion picture companies make an accurate transcription of it. It deals with evildoing without remorse…. It is the hardest-boiled of the hard-boiled yarns… . Bill is evil incarnate…. if we get many more books like this, will we become even more calloused, more indifferent than we are? Is this story mere entertainment for you? Then I'm sorry for you.

British intellectual and author George Orwell famously anticipated these concerns in his 1944 essay "The Ethics of the Detective Story from Raffles to Miss Blandish" (now known as "Raffles and Miss Blandish"), in which he lamented the decline in popularity of the traditional "innocent" British crime thriller with its public school ethos of honor and fair play and the rise of what he deemed the pornographic and fascistic new school of crime fiction, as represented by James Hadley Chase's hit novel. Orwell saw in *Orchids* "a daydream appropriate to the totalitarian age," with its forthright worship of power and cruelty for their own sake and its reflection of the grim doctrine that might makes right. Were such books as Chase's to "acclimatize themselves in England, instead of being merely a half-understood import from America," Orwell observed, "there would be good grounds for dismay."

What would Orwell have made of *Kiss the Blood off My Hands*? Probably he would have discerned in it, much as he had in *No Orchids for Miss Blandish*, signs of the moral decline of the British nation. The novel opens with Butler's brutish bruiser of a protagonist, Bill Saunders, realizing he has just killed a pub bouncer with a single punch and nonchalantly allowing to himself: "maybe

I hit him a bit harder than I meant." In the novel's most memorable lines he observes of the scene of his crime: "The whole pub had dried up like a scab. The place was so quiet you could hear a cat mess." (Presumably the word "piss" was too strong a brew for the publishers.) On the run from the outraged onlookers, he forces his way into an attractive young woman's cheap one-room flat, warning her: "keep quiet or I'll smash you up." In his first few moments there he finds himself wishing the woman were a man, but not out of any whimsical notions of chivalry. "You can sock a man to teach him to keep quiet," Bill reasons, "but with a girl that would just be asking for noise." Upon realization that the woman— "the kid" as he terms her (her name is Jane)—"didn't look like a tart," however, he bemusedly reflects: "Somehow or other I wouldn't have liked to have smashed the kid's face for her."

So begins a very strange relationship indeed, but hardly one unknown within the annals of criminal psychology. Jane, who by all appearances is a decent and upright human being, an honest little shopgirl in a provincial English city, is unaccountably attracted to Bill and does not squeal on him to the police. She tries her best to tame his brutal impulses with the proverbial good woman's love. This is where it might be argued that the book succumbs to sentimentality, setting it on a rather more of a primrose path than James M. Cain's *Postman*, yet Bill's seemingly innate viciousness keeps us nervously on our heels. Is Bill really remotely reformable? What will happen as the pressures pile up and up upon his big, broad shoulders?

More really cannot be said. The closing chapters indeed bear a strong resemblance to *Postman*, though the dénouement diverges significantly from the earlier novel. Critics of the day debated the meaning of Butler's enigmatic ending. The author himself suggestively observed: "I spend a considerable time over [my book] titles.... Look at *Kiss the Blood off My Hands*—surely that [title] implies the redemption of the guilty?" Not all critics agreed with him that his novel lived up to this hopeful implication.

Disappointingly, considering the huge sales which Butler's debut novel generated, the author earned from the book only about £1000, or £51,000 today (about 64,000 dollars). To the press he placed the blame for this inequitable windfall on "wartime costs" of production and distribution. Still, many a struggling author would have envied Butler his "disappointment." Striking while the poker was hot, he left the advertising business and devoted the decade of the Forties to fiction writing. Counting *Blood*, he produced, as mentioned above, four novels during the war years 1940 to 1945, three of which were published in the United States. At a slower rate two more novels in the Cain vein came from his hand in the postwar years, *Slippery Hitch* (1948) and *Blow Hot, Blow Cold* (1951), both of which were reprinted in the United States, with paperback editions as well. At this point, however, the well of inspiration ran dry: Butler would publish only one more, little heralded novel, over two decades later, in 1972.

The years following World War Two also saw Butler's involvement in the British film industry. He wrote the scripts for the thriller *The Fatal Night* (1948), adapted from Michael Arlen's twisty ghost story "The Gentleman from America," (1925) and for *Third Time Lucky* (1949), an adaptation of his own novel *They Cracked Her Glass Slipper* (1941). Additionally in 1948 and 1951 *Kiss the Blood off My Hands* and *Mad with Much Heart* were adapted as critically-praised American noir-inflected films, the latter under the title *On Dangerous Ground* and starring Robert Ryan and Ida Lupino.

The film version of *Blood* starred Americans Burt Lancaster and Joan Fontaine as Bill and Jane with heavily mugging Britisher Robert Newton as cockney diabolus-ex-machina Harry Carter. Predictably the film tempers the coarseness and brutality of the novel, turning it more into a romantic melodrama with noirish elements. The script fashionably attempts to make Bill more sympathetic to viewers by transforming him into a troubled combat veteran and former prisoner-of-war, where in the book Butler had provided readers with no such salves to tender consciences, leaving Bill's background a complete and utter blank. Both thirty-year-old Joan Fontaine as "the kid" and Burt Lancaster seem too intelligent and sophisticated for these characters. (Jane has even been upgraded from a hat shop assistant to a nurse.)

The film's ending especially is a cop-out, piously turning the book's ending on its head. Yet film critics gave it mostly positive reviews, while a more spiritually faithful version, as it were, likely would have appalled them and received pans, as had happened the previous year in the case of the film *Born to Kill*, which had been fairly and bravely adapted from James Gunn's raw and perverse crime novel *Deadlier Than the Male* (1942) (recently reprinted by Stark House). The most controversial thing about the film version of *Blood* was its memorably gory title, which theaters in some puritanical Middle American towns squeamishly altered to *The Unafraid*.

Over the rest of the twentieth century British reviewers never quite lost their frequent distaste for violent American crime fiction, however much the lay public on both sides of the Atlantic ate up such stuff on a bloody platter. Influential English critic Julian Symons, who viewed Jim Thompson condescendingly, was horrified by Mickey Spillane and positively disgusted by James Ellroy, predictably was dismissive of Cheyney and Chase, though Butler lucked out by going unmentioned in all three editions of Symons' genre survey *Bloody Murder*. The author had in fact sunk deep into obscurity. In 1987 an agent with the firm of Curtis Brown placed an ad in the London *Daily Telegraph* requesting that "anyone knowing the whereabouts of Gerald Butler, author of *Kiss the Blood off My Hands*, or his heirs" get in touch with her. It seemed American paperback publisher Carroll & Graf wanted to reprint the novel, which they did later that year, dubbing it on the front cover "the hard-boiled crime classic." This was Butler's last hurrah as an author. He died less than a year after *Blood*'s much-belated republication, on February 1, 1988, at the age of eighty. After yet another lapse, this time of nearly forty years, Stark House has rescued the novel from oblivion yet again. Gerald Butler's hands are bloody once more.

—March 2024
Memphis, TN

Curtis Evans received a PhD in American history in 1998. He is the author of *Masters of the "Humdrum" Mystery: Cecil John Charles Street, Freeman Wills Crofts, Alfred Walter Stewart and British Detective Fiction, 1920-1961* (2012), *Clues and Corpses: The Detective Fiction and Mystery Criticism of Todd Downing* (2013), *The Spectrum of English Murder: The Detective Fiction of Henry Lancelot Aubrey-Fletcher and G. D. H. and Margaret Cole* (2015) and editor of the Edgar nominated *Murder in the Closet: Essays on Queer Clues in Crime Fiction Before Stonewall* (2017). He writes about vintage crime fiction at his blog The Passing Tramp and at Crimereads.

KISS THE BLOOD OFF MY HANDS

GERALD BUTLER

Chapter One: A LUCKY DIP

By the time I've been blotting up beer for a couple of hours, any fellow who starts anything with me is crazy. Although maybe I hit him a bit harder than I meant, or maybe he hit his head as he went over, or something, but he looked like a chap who would want plenty of jab, and that isn't the way he looks as he's on the floor. He looks pretty still. He looks damned still. Come to think of it he looks too damned still.

The whole pub had dried up like a scab. The place was so quiet you could have heard a cat mess.

I rubbed my knuckles. Maybe I had hit him harder than I meant.

Nobody did anything. Doing anything was up to the bouncer. But the bouncer was on the floor, and didn't look as if he would be doing anything for quite a time.

"You certainly caught him one, mister," someone said at last.

I swung around fiercely, but the sucker shrunk away.

"What the hell's the good of hitting 'em if you don't hit 'em?" I asked.

Nobody said anything. Everybody stood looking at the bouncer on the floor. A trickle of blood had started coming from his mouth as he went down, but it had given up coming now. He'd got the look all right. I prodded him with my foot. He'd got the look all right. He'd got the look you don't usually have unless you've got a hole through you.

The beer started to go out of me.

"He ain't moving much," somebody said.

I could hear my own breath in the silence. The darts game had stopped. People had backed away, and a ragged circle had formed itself round us. A fellow came out of the crowd and got down on his knees, put his hand inside the bouncer's coat, and held it there. He got up looking scared and awkward.

"What's he like?" somebody asked.

"He's not breathing," said the feeler.

There was quiet for a minute, and then somebody whispered, "He's dead!"

Nobody did anything.

Then somebody else said, "He's dead!"

This time they said it a bit louder, and then someone who was three parts sozzled said it again, a hell of a lot louder, with a sort of scream to wrap it up.

"You killed him, mister," said somebody.

As I turned round on him to shut his mouth, somebody from the other side of the room said, "Fetch the police!" I stopped just an inch from the first fellow's face. This was a sucker's place to start another scrap. The bouncer was beginning to look lousy.

I turned for the door. It was ten yards away from me, the other end of the bar, with two fellows right in the way. But the place was hot, and there was no more time for talking. The beer was right out of my head now. I measured the distance, and went for the door with a rush, knocking the two mugs over without waiting for them to move. I pulled the door open and dived through it into the street.

The pub was on a corner, and the door I came out of was in a side street. The main road was a few yards to the left. I turned right, heading as fast as I could up the side street away from the main road.

I'd have said it would have taken those suckers in the pub ten minutes to make up their minds to do anything, but I couldn't have noticed some of them. As I came to the next corner there was a shout behind me, and the clatter of people running.

The beer was getting out of me now. I knew I could throw them off without much trouble, but I had turned into a long street that had no turnings out of it until you got right to the other end. Before I was halfway up it, a knot of people were round the corner trailing me. I was gaining fast, with a fifty-yard lead, but a copper strolling along on his beat took up the chase a bare twenty-five yards behind. Most of the slobs can't run, but this one could. I got to the end of the street and ducked to the left. It was beginning to warm up now. Glancing over my shoulder, I could see a chap on a bicycle shooting up to head me off. I ran off the pavement into the road, and as his front wheel drew level with me, I suddenly stopped dead and brought my shoulder thud into the side of his body. He spun across the road, and the crash of metal followed me as I started running again.

Turning another corner, I found myself in a main road. A bus was just drawing away from its stopping-place, and I jumped on it as it gathered speed. But I hadn't got a good enough lead. The conductor was coming down the steps as I landed on it, and he saw the hounds just coming round the corner. He gave me one look and put up his hand for the bell. I gave him one in the belly, and jumped off into the gutter as the bus checked speed. I had gained a bit; there was nearly a hundred yards now between me and the panting crowd behind.

I ducked down a side street and got going in earnest, but the beer was in my bladder now. Just two minutes' pause and I could have run them all off their feet, but with the beer where it was, it wasn't any fun.

I put on a spurt and went around a couple of quick corners to try and lose them, but I was out of luck. The beer was getting pretty awkward now. I had got to stop, but I couldn't. I clenched my fists and tightened myself a bit. I ran like a madman for two or three more streets, and just as the beer was ready to burst me I rounded a corner and saw a girl going into a door. I shot up the four or five steps and reached the door just before she shut it. Pushing it open again, I slid through and slammed it behind the two of us.

The girl still had her keys in her hand. She took one quick, bewildered look at me, and made up her mind. Darting to a door on the right of the hall, she put a key in the lock, pushed the door open, snatched the key out again, and went to shut the door in my face. But I was too quick for her. I pushed her into the room and closed the door quietly behind us.

"Shut up and keep quiet," I said.

She did not make a sound. She gaped at me, too surprised to say anything. I could see her clearly, because the curtains were not drawn and the street lamp was shining right into the room.

"Don't put the light on," I told her. "And keep quiet or I'll smash you up."

She stood there, perfectly still, as the noise in the street came closer. The crowd had got to the corner now, and they were running around in circles, shouting and blaming each other.

They must have guessed I had ducked in somewhere. There was a bit of talking, and then I could hear them starting to hammer on the doors. Soon they were hammering on the door that I had come through. I got hold of the girl's wrist and turned it a bit, and brought my other fist close to her face.

"Better keep quiet," I whispered.

There were footsteps on the stairs, and then a shuffling in the hall, and I heard the front door being opened.

"Anyone just come in here?" a voice panted.

"Who do you want to see?" The woman who had come downstairs sounded the kind of person who spent her life keeping people out of places.

"We're looking for a man who just disappeared round this corner. He was trying to escape. Must have come into one of these houses."

The woman's voice became more haughty than ever.

"Are you suggesting that this house is run for the benefit of people who are trying to escape? Get along with you! Let me tell you that some people in this world are respectable, even if some others are not. Please get off my doorstep at once!"

"No offense, lady—but we've got to find this chap. Didn't anyone just come in here?"

"Certainly not! The idea! How dare you suggest that I am accommodating your—er—your associates!"

The front door shut with a bang, and with a final outraged "Huh!" the woman shuffled back up the stairs.

The girl was still standing quiet. By the light from the street lamp I looked round the room. It was a sort of everything rolled into one. There was a bed, and an armchair, and a gas ring, and a washbasin.

I let go her wrist.

"Stand facing that corner," I told her, pointing to the corner on the left of the fireplace.

That bag upstairs would be all ears now. I didn't dare go along the passage looking for what I wanted, so I went over to the washbasin, humming softly to try and cover up. When I had finished I went back to the girl and turned her round.

"Excuse me, kid," I said. "It was better than busting."

She didn't say anything. She just looked at me, so straight that I couldn't make her out. She was neatly dressed, not flashy. She didn't look like a tart.

"Go on keeping quiet," I told her, but there didn't seem to be any need.

I went over to the window and looked out. The place was clearing off now. The crowd were right up the road, still talking and arguing. I drew the curtains carefully, found the light switch and put on the light.

The girl was pretty. Her eyes were bright, and somewhere around her mouth there was a curious tilt that made her look all the time as if she was just going to smile. I wished to hell she was a man. You can sock a man to teach him to keep quiet, but with a girl that would be just asking for noise.

"This isn't a push around," I told her. "Don't be scared."

"Don't flatter yourself," she answered. "Who frightened you?"

"Nobody frightens me," I started, but I stopped because she must be kidding.

"Who are you running away from, then?"

"Don't ask me questions," I said. "Just you keep nice and quiet and you'll be all right. The wisest thing for you to do right now is to keep nice and quiet."

"What if I don't?"

Somehow or other I just wouldn't have liked to have smashed that kid's face for her. I tried to keep the thing friendly by answering her question.

"I was just running away from a fellow," I said vaguely. "Just running away from a fellow because I don't want to see him."

"It seemed to me as if that fellow was a dozen fellows," she said.

I grinned at her.

"You're right, kid. There were at least a dozen, and I didn't want to see any of them."

"Very interesting!" she said, getting a cigarette from her handbag, lighting it, and blowing the smoke out very deliberately.

"And now I suppose you will have to be tearing yourself away?" she asked.

I shook my head emphatically.

"You've got it wrong there, kid," I said. "I guess those mugs will take a long time clearing off."

Anyone is only too anxious to forget a bit of trouble usually, but that used-up bouncer was going to take a bit of getting off their minds. I guessed they would have people snooping around the district all night.

"You've got it wrong there, kid," I said again. "I wasn't thinking of pushing off just yet."

She raised her eyebrows, acting.

"Indeed? And how long were you considering extending your stay?"

"Don't poke me," I said. "I'm staying here the night, and you had better get used to the idea."

"Charming!" she exclaimed, and moved suddenly toward the door with her hand up for the handle. She was a quick mover, light on her feet, but I caught her just in time. I grabbed her arm, flung her round onto the bed, and put my hand on her throat to stop her from squawking.

"Listen, kid," I said, and looked her straight in the face. "Listen carefully. If I've got to choose between getting out of this room now and doing something that will make you keep quiet, I don't go out of the room, see?"

For the first time she looked a bit scared. I took my hand off her throat; the flesh was red. I must have pinched it more than I meant, but it had certainly done a lot to get her tame. For a flimsy bit of a girl she had good guts. But now she was lying on the bed looking up at me as if she couldn't quite make up her mind.

"You're going to be all right," I told her "You just put off the light and carry on as if you had never seen or heard of me. I'll squat down on the floor in this corner by the door, and wait till the morning."

Her eyes were fixed on me as I spoke, as if she was trying to size me up. She lay there without moving, just where I had thrown her. The white of her neck was still flushed where my hand had been. For what seemed like minutes she lay there, looking at me steadily. Then at last she appeared to have made up her mind. Still without speaking, she rolled her body half over on the bed, and turned her head away from me.

I switched off the light, and sat down on the floor in the corner, leaning my back against the wall. The house was quiet, and it was quiet now outside. The hue and cry had died right down, but the odds were they would still be snooping about somewhere. I would have to do some thinking when the morning came. There wasn't much doubt about that bouncer. He'd got the look all right. That was just his bad luck, but it might turn out to be mine. I had got to watch out that it didn't turn out to be mine.

But I was tired, and that could wait till morning. This place was good for the night. It had been a lucky dip. She wouldn't squawk, not tonight. She would have done it by now if she meant to do it tonight. The room was for one, so there shouldn't be anyone else butting in before morning. Not then, very likely, because there were cups and plates and tins on the shelf, as if she looked after her own breakfast. This place was a snip, and the thinking could wait till the morning.

I shifted myself and got as comfortable as I could in the corner. After about an hour, the heavy breathing from the bed told me that she had dropped off to sleep. I settled down to keep myself awake, but the beer and the running had made me tired, and after a bit I started dozing.

I woke up at the sound of milk bottles being put outside the front door. Daylight was coming in through a gap in the curtains, and I reckoned it must be getting on for seven.

It sounded as if the kid was asleep. I got up, feeling stiff and cramped, and went on tiptoe across to the window and looked out through the curtains. It was raining. From the window end of the room I could see her face, and she was still asleep right enough. She hadn't undressed. It looked as if she hadn't moved.

I looked around the room for something to gag her with. If she woke up and suddenly saw me, she might let out a yell before she had time to collect her wits. But then I looked at her neck, where even now it was still a bit red from where I had squashed it, and I decided to risk it. So far she hadn't shown up to be the squawking kind.

I prodded her. She opened her eyes and looked at me without moving, just as if she had been expecting to see me there all the time.

"I want to talk to you," I said.

She raised herself up and sat on the bed, rubbing her eyes and yawning. She looked down at her clothes, then looked over into the corner by the door, and then looked back at me.

"Still here?"

"I want to talk to you," I said.

"Go ahead," she said. "You seem to please yourself."

"Do you live here alone?" I asked her.

"I thought I did," she answered. She was awake all right.

"Anybody come to get breakfast or do the room out?" I asked her. She shook her head.

"I am afraid I can't offer you service," she said.

"Stop poking me," I told her. "I'm serious. I'm not in here because I like the place, or because I think I can stand you for long. I'm here because I've got to hide up for a bit, see? And you're going to help me!"

"You seem to know," she said.

"What do you do all day?" I asked her.

"Mind your own business!" she snapped.

"What do you do?" I asked her, slower this time. She changed her mind.

"I work at Benny's," she said.

"Who's Benny?"

"Benny's is a shop. I thought everyone knew that."

"I'm different," I said. "I've only been in this town a couple of days. When do you have to go to work?"

"I leave in about an hour," she said, and looked at me as if it were a challenge.

I lit a cigarette and gave her one. We sat there smoking, facing each other, like a couple of fighting cats having a breather. It was an awkward situation, and I couldn't quite figure out how to handle it. I wasn't in any hurry to show out in the street, in case they were still snooping round. And yet if I bottled her up in this room, there might be people nosing around to know what was up with her.

To ease the situation I jerked my thumb toward the shelves. "What about some coffee?" I asked her.

Still smoking her cigarette, she went over to the mirror by the washbasin, and pushed her hair about a bit and looked at her face.

Then she turned toward me again, gave me another long sizing-up look, and seemed to make up her mind. She got the kettle off the gas ring, filled it with water at the basin, and put it back on. She got down a couple of cups and saucers from the shelf and started to put some coffee in the pot.

"Milk's by the front door," she said.

I smiled. "We'll drink it black," I told her.

She looked at me hard for a minute, and then said quietly, "I'll fetch it and come back."

I looked at her straight. We had got to come to it soon. I looked right into her eyes, but they didn't move.

"All right," I said.

She went across the room and opened the door and went out into the hall. I tightened myself and listened. As she opened the front door I heard footsteps coming along the street. They were slow, steady footsteps, just about level with the house. I was right on my toes by now, and I felt my hands tightening.

The milk bottle clinked against the step, and the front door shut again. I could hear the footsteps passing on along the street. When she had come back into the room and shut the door behind her, she gave me a funny kind of look. I jerked my head questioningly in the direction of the street. She nodded.

I tried to puzzle her out as she made the coffee. But reasons didn't seem to fit in anywhere. She filled the two cups, handed one to me without saying a word, and then sat down in the armchair and stirred the sugar in hers. I sat down on the edge of the bed facing her, and tried to get the whole thing clearer in my mind.

"Look," I said, after we had sat there in silence for a while. "Look— we'd better get this clear. I've got to hide in here until those mugs have stopped looking for me, see? Now, you're a good kid, but all the same, what was to stop me bashing you up last night? Nothing! But I didn't do it, and do you know why? I didn't do it because—"

She cut right in on me. "Don't trouble!" she said. "You seem to imagine that as long as you go on using this ridiculous bullying language, I shall be forced to do exactly what you tell me. Now look at it this way. You came bursting in here last night, scared out of your wits. No, don't interrupt—people don't run away and hide in strange people's rooms unless they are scared, do they? You came bursting in here, and for some reason which I cannot for the life of me explain, I allowed you to stay. I don't know why I did it, but I suppose everyone does something completely extraordinary once in a while. Anyway, here you still are. And here, apparently, you hope to stay for a few more hours. Well, just let me point something out to you, in case it hasn't occurred to you. I am due at work very soon. If I don't turn up, they will think I am ill and one of my friends will come running round in the lunch hour on an errand of mercy. Then you will have two people to deal with. Also, if you keep me here against my will, I can scream any moment I choose to, and soon have someone rushing in to help."

She paused to take a gulp of coffee, but before I could get started she went on quickly again.

"The alternative is for me to go out, and you to stay here. Would I trust you, I wonder? Yes, I think I would. For one thing, if you had come here to steal, you would have done it by now. And for another thing, I think it would be rather amusing. Do you know why it would be amusing? Because it would really be you who was having to trust me. All day long you would be saying to yourself, 'I wonder if she has told anyone yet. Are the police on their way yet?' I think that would be very amusing, don't you? Of course, if you prefer to go out now, you can. Or if you want to hear how loud I can scream, all you have to do is try to keep me in here!"

She had rattled it all off at full speed, and now she stopped, rather out of breath.

I went on gaping at her for a minute. Her nerve looked like being a nuisance. I ought to have gagged her before she woke up. Now it would mean a scrap.

"You've got a lot of talk," I said, "but where do you think it gets you? I don't ask for favors, kid. I take them."

She didn't answer. She just looked. I couldn't remember ever seeing a girl so sure of herself.

"Are you telling me, kid, that if I let you out of this room you're going to squawk?"

She shrugged her shoulders.

"I didn't say so," she said. And then there was that funny kind of look again, and she held out the milk bottle.

"Have some more—milk?" she asked.

I looked at the milk bottle, and heard the clink of it on the doorstep, and heard the footsteps that had gone straight on along the street.

"Okay!" I said.

She got up and stood by the washbasin near the window, and pointed to the far wall.

"Go and admire the wallpaper," she said.

I went over and sat on the bed facing the wall. Something whistled over my head, and yesterday's newspaper dropped at my feet. I picked it up and started to look at it.

She was tidying up, getting ready for the day. I could hear the running of water, and then after a bit—I think she hesitated a bit—I could hear the rustle of clothes coming off.

"Don't look around," she said.

"Don't worry," I told her.

That was easy enough for me. That kind of thing never did anything to me. There was a place and a time for that with me, and there was a kind of woman to do it with, and that kind of woman wasn't her.

I turned the paper over. They were looking for a fellow who had cut up a body in bits. They were looking for a girl who had stuck a knife into her sweetheart. They were looking for a fellow who—

It seemed to be getting a bit personal. The paper was full of accounts of the police looking for somebody who had finished with somebody else. Papers always were, but you didn't notice it much as long as you didn't happen to know the people. I wondered what today's would have to say.

"Hey, kid!" I said over my shoulder.

"M-m-m?"

"Will you do something for me?"

"I thought you decided that," she said.

"Ease up," I said. "Will you get me the papers when you are out?"

"You are getting easy! Which one do you want?"

"All of them," I said.

She laughed. "Want to try and decide which one to believe?"

"I'm serious," I said. "Will you bring them all back with you?"

"Anything to oblige," she said. "You can stop admiring the wallpaper now."

I turned round. She had changed her clothes, and was wearing quite a different get-up now, but she still had the same tidy neatness. Her fair hair, spruced up for the day, caught the light from the window, glinting as she moved. Her face still had the curious tilt which made her look all the time as if she was just going to smile. I couldn't remember when I had seen a girl who looked less of a nuisance.

I pulled out a bundle of notes and tossed a pound on the bed.

"Take the papers out of that," I said. "And get me some cigarettes, will you?"

Her eyes followed the roll back into my pocket, and then went down to the pound note. She looked surprised, but she didn't say anything.

"What time are you going to be back?" I asked.

"About seven, if I'm lucky."

"You don't come back midday?"

She shook her head. "That's when someone else does my cooking for a change," she said. She pulled on her hat, picked up her handbag, and moved toward the door.

"Wait a minute!" I said. "Have you got any cigarettes you can leave behind?"

She opened her bag, pulled out a half-used packet, and tossed it onto the bed. She went to move toward the door again.

"Wait a minute!" I said, and took hold of her wrist, but not to hurt it. I looked at her straight. "Is this a go?" I asked her.

She looked at me for a minute, and then she said, "I don't think I would do it that way, anyhow. I shouldn't be here to see the fun."

"Why are you doing this?" I asked her.

She hesitated, and then she suddenly turned and pulled the door open.

"Don't ask impossible questions!" she said, and went out and slammed the door behind her.

I went over to the window and looked out. She was walking quickly up the street. There were several other people about, but she didn't speak to anybody. I wondered if the snoopers were still hanging round. There was no sign of anyone watching, but if that bouncer was as cold as he had looked, they wouldn't be giving the chase up yet. It was just as well to wait indoors for a bit longer.

The kid was nearly at the end of the street. I watched her go round the corner, and then turned away from the window. I took out a penny and spun it up and it came down tails on the carpet, but I hadn't called. There was something about her. I picked up a magazine and settled down to wait.

It was dark when she came back. As she opened the door, I got behind it and bunched up my hand ready to fix anyone who came in with her. But she came in alone and I felt a bit silly. She shut the door and plonked a bundle of newspapers on the bed. Then she drew a couple of packages of cigarettes out of her handbag.

"Still here?" she asked.

"Still here!" I said, and started to go through the papers.

It was there all right. His name was Martin, and there hadn't been any mistake about him. There never is when they look like that.

Three of the papers had got it on the front page, and they had painted it up good and hard. I read the accounts through carefully.

I was a dago. I was a sailor. I was an all-in wrestler. I was almost every damned thing, and the fight had been the hell of a fight, and several fellows had grabbed me and tried to hold me back. The hell they had! The hell, they hadn't touched me! Those gaping suckers wouldn't have tried to hold me back and still be talking big.

I turned round to the kid. "Did you see about this showdown?" I said offhand.

"What showdown?" she asked.

"This scrap where the dago slogged the barman."

"Oh, yes," she said.

"And this one where the dago was a sailor?"

"What do you mean?"

I grinned. "Perhaps the one you saw was the one where the sailor was an all-in wrestler?"

She put down the plates she had in her hand and came over and faced me.

"Go on," she said quietly.

"Go on? But you said you'd read it," I said. "I was just gossiping about the day's news."

She gave me a strange, searching look.

"In half a dozen papers," she said slowly, "there's more news than one fight in a pub. How long does it take to get from there to here?"

I tightened up. "I don't know what you're talking about!" I said.

She went on looking hard at me, standing absolutely still. I cursed myself inside. But trying to fool her wouldn't be like fooling any ordinary person.

I shrugged my shoulders.

"So long!" I said.

"Going?"

I nodded.

"It's foggy outside," she said.

"Foggy suits me fine!" I answered.

"Here's your change." She held out a ten-shilling note and some coins. I was just going to tell her to keep it, but I changed my mind. She wasn't a money-box girl. I took it and put it in my pocket, and moved over toward the door.

"Thanks for everything," I said.

She didn't answer. I took a long look at her, and then I went out into the passage and closed the door quietly behind me. I opened the front door and went out into the street, and walked off quickly into what was quite a fog.

Chapter Two: TAXI-RIDER

It was good to be on the move again. After a whole day of not doing anything I always felt like a dried-up fig, so I walked along at a good pace, swinging my arms and feeling like something that had just escaped from somewhere.

The fog was patchy, very thick in places. I walked so fast that several times I cannoned into people. One mug, groping round a corner, put himself right square in the way, and the biff sent him sprawling in the gutter. I heard him shouting after me, but I was feeling so good with being moving again that I couldn't be bothered to stop and knock silence into him. I walked on and on, not caring where, just enjoying stretching myself.

There didn't seem much to worry about. Those papers the kid had brought home with her had changed the look of things a lot. In the general excitement, nobody could have taken a very careful look at me. Every paper had a different description. Even their accounts of what had happened didn't tally. Some of them talked about it as if it had been a general scrap, with everybody in the pub having a go. There certainly wasn't a single description that would help anybody to recognize me. As long as they didn't know who they were looking for, they could go on looking as long as they liked without it bothering me.

The fog was clearing a bit, but it was going to be a stinking night. I felt like sleeping out, but the weather didn't fit. I walked on, crossing a batch of evening-dress streets, and came to a big, quiet square where every building seemed to be a hotel. They were not the kind that want to see your luggage, but the ones that grab you with open arms if you've got the six-and-sixpence.

I turned into one of them.

"I want a room for tonight," I told the woman.

"For one, sir?"

"That's all," I said.

"Any luggage?"

"No."

"That will be five shillings without breakfast," she said. "Do you mind paying in advance?"

I gave her the money.

"I will show you the room," she said.

"Don't bother," I said, "just tell me the number." She told me seventeen.

"Back later," I said. The gloom of the place was more than you could stand for eating in.

I went out into the street again to look for a feed. Just off the square there was a restaurant that looked quite cozy. It was rather crowded and I couldn't see an empty table, so I sat down at a table where there were four seats but only two of them taken. The two men at the table had finished their meal and were sitting smoking cigarettes over their empty coffee cups.

I had finished a plate of soup and was just starting the meat when one of them said something that made me sit up with a jolt. He was talking about me. He was talking about the slogging that I had given the bouncer in the pub.

"I wonder if they've caught that bullying lout who did it?" one of them said.

Bullying lout! I put down my knife and fork. My hands bunched up and tightened, and my teeth came together with a snap. But I stopped myself in time. They might think I had an interest in the thing if I did that. Some people are always ready to put things together too quickly.

"You know the pub, don't you?" said one of the men. "It was the one just round the corner."

I nearly choked on my beef. Like a fool I had gone round in a circle and come back to the one spot in this town that was likely to be unhealthy.

Without waiting to finish the meal, I got up from the table, paid the bill, and left the restaurant quickly. Out in the street I paused for a moment, wondering round which corner the pub was. As I stood there, suddenly the fog lifted, and from round the first corner to the right came the leisurely form of a copper. Turning my back, I walked away as quickly as I could without looking to be in a hurry.

When I got up in the morning and looked in the mirror, it was a ragged sight. I hadn't shaved for a couple of days. And what with getting a bit wet, and being slept in the night before, my suit was looking like hell.

I pressed the bell in the bedroom, and when the girl came up I told her to bring me breakfast in the room. While she was fetching it, I found a bathroom and had a wash down, but having no razor I had to leave the stubble on.

As soon as I had eaten the breakfast, I went downstairs and paid the extra for the food and left the hotel. Turning in the direction opposite from the restaurant where I had been the evening before, I walked briskly for a mile or more, feeling that one of the first things to do was to get clear of that district. The next thing to do was to get a spruce up, so I dropped into a barber's shop and had a shave.

After I had paid for that, I counted my money and found that I had just over seven pounds. That was not much of a reserve, and it would need building up pretty quickly. The town was a stranger to me, and so far I hadn't had time to find out where the money hung around. It seemed to be time for taxi-riding, which was always good for several quid a night in any decent, respectable town. But my suit was looking like hell, and if you are going to do taxi-riding you've got to look the part.

I decided to invest what money I had in getting myself a bit of flash. So I walked along until I came to a shop that sold clothes. I went in and told them I wanted a suit. The assistant smirked.

"You wish to be measured for a suit, sir?" he asked.

"No," I said, "I want it now. I want a suit, a shirt, a tie, and a hat, and I want them for seven quid."

He brought out three suits to show me, and I chose one and tried it on. It didn't look bad. I looked at myself in a glass and it looked pretty good.

"I'll have this," I told him.

"Shall I send it?" he asked.

"No," I said. "Where's the shirt and tie?"

He produced some shirts. I took off the one I was wearing, screwed it up, and chucked it on the counter, and put on one of the new ones. Then I fixed a tie, put the new suit on again, and emptied the pockets of my old one.

"How much?" I asked.

"The suit is six guineas and the shirt ten-and-six and the tie two-and-six, that is six pounds nineteen."

"I'll do without the hat," I said, and handed him my seven pounds.

"Are you wearing that now, sir?" he asked.

"Use your eyes," I told him.

"Where shall I send your other suit?"

"Anywhere you like," I said, and came out into the street.

I was all set up now, and looking pretty good. All I needed now was a guide-map of the town and a bit of darkness. I bought the map, and then found a restaurant and had a good lunch. This left me with only a few coppers, but I was all set now.

I walked off and found a park, and sat down on a seat to study the guide-map and wait for it to get dark. Taxi-riding was a good way of getting started in a new town, but I had always believed in playing on a sound geography basis. If you don't do that, there's a risk of doubling back on your own tracks by mistake, and getting off just where the cops are on the lookout. So I fixed the layout of the main streets carefully in my mind, and then sat and watched the nursemaids pushing their prams around and the old ladies feeding the pigeons, and waited for the light to go.

As soon as it was dusk I moved off to look for the flash streets. By the time I reached them it was properly dark, and I strolled along casually until I came to a taxi rank. About twenty yards ahead of the front taxi I ducked in a doorway to wait. After a few minutes a man with a girl came along and hailed the front cab. Then a man came along alone and took the next one, but I let him go because he looked too tough to start on. You get warmed up to this kind of thing, but you want to start on something easy.

Soon enough a fellow who said mug all over him came along and waggled his umbrella. He told the driver where he wanted to go, and got in and shut the door, and the cabby started up his engine.

Just as it was about to move off, I was alongside the cab, opening the door and grinning like a long-lost friend.

"Hullo, old man! Where have you been hiding yourself?" I asked him cheerfully. The mug gaped.

"I'm afraid—" he started in an awkward tone, but I covered it up with "Right you are, carry on, cabby!" and slammed the door behind me. The cabby drove off without troubling to look round twice. I was looking the part all right.

"You have made a mistake," the mug was starting, but I shut him up.

"Listen!" I said. "Did you ever go to the pictures and see one of those nasty films where the sucker slumps out of a taxicab like a lump of dung? That's what happens to you any minute now if you don't keep quiet. Just make a sound, or rap on the window, or do any damn thing, and you're finished. This is just to show you!"

I short-jabbed him in the face, and then clamped my hand quickly over his mouth, because he looked like the kind that might yelp when you hit him. But he was easy. He was such a soft mug that it was almost like robbing a blind baby.

"Turn out your pockets!" I told him.

He gaped as if I didn't make sense.

"Your money," I said, and slapped him again just to wake him up a bit. He looked such a frightened mug I could have spewed on him.

He shook like a jelly and pulled out his notecase. I grabbed it and moved back across the seat to give myself room. Then I brought my right fist over in a real lovely jab. He sagged on the seat like a lump of nothing. I shoved the notecase in my pocket, and rapped on the front window. As the cab slowed down, I opened the door and put my head out to catch the cabby's attention before he looked into the cab.

"Drop me here—the other fellow's going on to where he said," I told him.

Before the taxi had quite stopped I hopped on the curb and slammed the door.

"Cherrio, old man!" I shouted. "See you later!"

The cab drove on and I strolled along the pavement until it was out of sight. Then I dropped into the first bar I came to and ordered a drink. I pulled the mug's notecase out of my pocket to get some money to pay. There was five pounds ten shillings in it. I changed the ten-shilling note and shoved the five one-pound notes into my trouser pocket. Then I swallowed the drink and went out into the street again.

I walked along until I came to a bin for litter, and tossed the empty notecase into it.

Carefully checking up the names of the streets, I marked with a pencil on my map a black circle round the spot where I had got out of the taxi. That was the beginning of the evening's danger zone. That was where the taxi driver would say I had hopped out, and any time now special snoopers would be hanging around that area. I had to be careful not to start or finish another ride in that circle.

Walking briskly for ten minutes, I picked on another taxi rank and took up my position again in a doorway. I had to wait quite a time before a suitable fare came along, but when it did come it was even easier than the first. That was always the best of a big town. The bigger the town, the softer the mugs. After a couple of hours' work, there was close on to twenty pounds in my pocket. But the map had a good many circles penciled on it, and I reckoned it was time to pack up for the evening.

It wasn't at all a bad start for a new town, and I wandered off to have some food and a drink to celebrate. It was a lovely night and there were a lot of people on the streets. I walked along idly, looking for a restaurant, turning away from the bright streets into the quieter ones. A tart grinned at me and I scowled back. I went into a bar and had a drink or two. There were snacks laid out temptingly on the counter, and I sat on a stool and ate there.

When I came out, I found the same tart was walking along just in front of me. Her skirt was drawn tight around her, and she waggled her bottom deliberately. As I came up to her she bumped against me lightly, and said something to me.

"Well, what?" I asked her.

"Have you got any money to spend on a naughty girl?" she asked.

I was certainly looking the part all right.

"What would you say?" I asked her.

"I'd say you'd got plenty," she said.

I grinned.

"You got a place?" I asked her.

"Just round the corner, dear," she said.

"Shut up talking!" I said. "I've got half an hour to waste."

"How much have you got? Three pounds?"

"I might spare one," I said.

"One? What do you take me for?"

I shrugged my shoulders. "Take it or leave it," I told her.

As we moved off she put her hand through my arm, but I rapped on her knuckles and she drew it away quick.

"All right," I said. "I didn't mean to hurt you."

She laughed. "Of course you didn't, dear," she said.

"How long have you been at it?" I asked.

"Long enough to know how to show you a good time all right, dear," she said.

"It's a funny thing," I said. "Does every woman take a turn at being a tart some time or other?"

"Don't call me a tart," she said.

"Why?"

"We don't like being called names, that's why."

"Who's we?"

"None of us girls don't like it."

I laughed.

"Don't you like doing it?" I asked her.

"It's nice when I get a nice gentleman like you," she smirked.

I stifled a belch and said, "Shut up talking."

She stopped at a doorway and took out a key and unlocked it.

"This way," she said. "I've got a nice flat up here."

We went in and she shut the door and switched on the light in the hall. It was nice enough in the hall. Then she started to lead the way upstairs. It's a funny thing, but with a tart there are always a lot of stairs.

We climbed right up to the top of the building. She took out another key and unlocked a door on the top landing. We went in, and she locked the door behind her.

"May I have the money, please?" she said.

I gave her one of the first mug's pound notes. She took it and put it in her handbag, and shut it up and put it on the mantelpiece. Then she took off her clothes so quickly you'd have thought she was racing someone.

"You don't look so good now," I told her.

"Come on, dear," she said. "Don't waste time talking. Let's see what a big, strong man you are."

We sprawled across the bed and it was soon over, and then she was off like a flash putting on her things again.

I lit a cigarette, and put on my jacket and did myself up, and watched her dress. It's a funny thing how there's nothing to it with tarts. It's simply like something that beer does to you, or else it's the way they waggle their tight-skirted bottoms in front of your eyes.

She was doing up her suspenders as I walked over to the mantelpiece and picked up her handbag.

"Excuse me, lady," I said.

"Put that down!" she flashed, and pounced across the room and grabbed the wrist of the hand I was holding the bag with. I twisted my wrist free and gave her a shove backward.

"Ease up," I told her. "You don't have to get excited. I won't take anything that doesn't belong to me. Not in somebody else's house," I explained.

"Give me that bag!" she said.

"You can have it in a minute," I told her. "I'm just going to take my pound out of it first, that's all."

She came at me in a fury now, and I jerked my head back just in time as her nails grazed down my cheek. Then I picked her up and chucked her right across the room onto the bed. She was so surprised she lay there and didn't know quite what to do. She couldn't yell; the landladies won't stand them if they yell.

"Yours is a pretty one-sided racket," I said. "But you've got to lose sometimes. You say it's your pound. I say it's mine. When it comes to a simple argument like that, you've got to lose sometimes."

"You've had what you wanted, haven't you?" she said fiercely. "Do you think you can come and maul me about for nothing?"

"That's your lookout," I told her. "I've never been out looking for a tart. I wasn't looking for you tonight. You started the whole thing up. You dangled yourself in front of me and started the whole thing. I don't blame you; you've got to advertise. You've got to dangle the smell under somebody's nose, but if the nose helps itself just once in a while, you can't whine about it."

I took the pound note out of the handbag and put the bag back on the mantelpiece. I thought she was going to fly at me again, but she didn't. Some of those landladies keep them pretty tame.

She had left the key in the lock, and I opened the door.

"You dirty sod!" she said in a low, spitty kind of voice. "You stinking bastard!"

I pulled myself up with the door half shut, but I let it go. One of the best ways to keep women happy is to let them call you things. She had been a nuisance anyhow. She had wasted good time that I might have spent in looking for somewhere to sleep. Women always were a nuisance. The kid hadn't been. That was funny; that kid could have been a hell of an extra nuisance, but she'd known how to behave all right.

I got to the bottom of the tart's stairs and came out into the street. I would have to start fixing myself up with a place somewhere. It was no good tramping around with no luggage to a different hotel each night, because the good ones wouldn't take you, and you had to put up with the cheap sheds like the one I had slept in last night. It was getting toward midnight now. It was a lovely night and I wandered off slowly in the direction of the park where I had been that afternoon. That would do me fine. That was always the best way to sleep if the weather was right. Apart from the risk of having your sleep interrupted by snoopers, it was a fine way to sleep.

I came down to where the park was, but the gates were shut. They probably shut it at dark, soon after I left it. So I walked along the railings for a bit until I came to a place where some trees threw a shadow on the railings. I looked up and down, but there was no one much about and I hopped over.

I walked across the grass to find the path, because the ground was none too dry, and one of the long seats would be better. When I came to the path there were about a dozen long seats by the side of it, but not one of them was empty. On some of them sprawled a man, or a woman; on others there were a couple of people propped up, one in each corner. They all looked like down-and-out mugs.

I went up to one of the seats where there was one mug lying right along it, and pulled his feet down and made room for myself.

"Here, come off it!" he said.

"Shut up!" I said.

He was dressed in ragged clothes and he looked pretty sick around the face.

"Is this place always cluttered up with mugs like these?" I asked him.

"We're here when we can get here," said the mug. "Where else d'you suggest, the Ritz Hotel? I wouldn't 've thought a toff like you needed a seat in the park."

"I don't need anything," I told him. "You mugs who lie around starving and shivering make me want to spew. I've eaten a good meal tonight. I've had plenty of beer tonight. I've got a new suit on. But nobody's given me anything. Here are you mugs in the middle of a town that stinks with money, and you slop around waiting for some of it to drop on your heads. You make me sick!"

"What do you mean, mister?" he asked.

"Shut up," I told him, "or I'll take the whole seat to myself."

I propped myself up in the corner, but the iron dug into my back. So after I had shifted about and tried it every way, I got off the seat and lay down on the asphalt path and slept soundly till morning.

Chapter Three: WITH HER IT'S DIFFERENT

The man in the secondhand luggage shop was an obliging fellow. From a junk shop nearby he fetched a pile of old magazines, and into the big suitcase that I had bought he put just enough to give it the right weighty feeling, just as if it were full of clothes, padding the spare space out with bunched-up newspaper to stop the magazines from sliding about. I paid him, lugged the suitcase out into the street, and called a taxi.

"Where's a good comfy hotel, middle price, not on a main street?" I asked him.

He told me Fletcher's. I got into the cab and told him to take me there. I booked a room, and left my suitcase there while I went out to buy a razor and a few odds and ends. When I had taken these back to the hotel, and laid them about the room so that it didn't look so bare, I went out to have a look around and get more acquainted with the town. So far, apart from that mess-up in the pub, this town was looking like working out in a nice friendly way. You never know with a town until you actually get there. Some towns you never seem to fit into the place, and with others you find your feet almost straight away. I felt I was going to be pretty good at this one. The last town, I never seemed to get the hang of at all. I even had to leave it pretty quick in the end. It's funny how they vary. Some places you find yourself scrapping half the time, just because the town doesn't happen to take to strangers. In others, they've got every way of making money so damned organized that you can't cut into anything without a lot of sweat and argument. But this was looking like a pretty good place. And anyway, the flat-racing season was just starting, and that was always an easier time.

I strolled along and looked at the people, and looked at the shops, and looked at everything there was. I dropped into a shop and bought myself a hat, and when I looked in the glass I could see that I looked the part all right. Along the street was a big open place that was full of slot machines. I never could resist those things. Every time there's a new kind I have to go on playing it and playing it, until they bring out another. I spent a few shillings in coppers, trying to get the five cigarettes that they were offering to anyone who beat five thousand. After a time it struck me that they had bent the pins too close together, so that to get the five cigarettes was just about more than the ten balls could do. I tried lifting up the machine so as to coax the balls slowly into place. You could do it better that way, and after a couple of goes like that, I beat the five thousand.

I flicked my fingers for the girl who was looking after the place. She came along, and I pointed to the score and grinned. She grinned back and pointed to a notice on the machine which said it had been tilted.

"Sorry, mister," she said.

She was a nasty, cocky little bitch.

"Give me those five cigarettes," I told her.

"Nothing doing," she said. "You tilted it, I saw you."

Her hand was resting on the machine, and I brought down my elbow hard on the back of it. She snatched it away and yelped a bit.

"Get out!" she said. "Get out or I'll have you thrown out!"

I laughed.

It was a time of day when a lot of people go to work, and there was no one else there except for a couple of pimply-faced, undersized mugs, who gave us a glance and started to edge away. There was no one else looking after the place, and I guessed that a part of her job was to keep the place nice and quiet and friendly. I looked along the row of machines, and then looked back at her and grinned.

"Lot of glass around here, in these machines," I pointed out.

She hesitated, and then took the hint. She put her hand in her apron pocket and fished out the packet of five cigarettes.

"Now get out," she said. "We don't want people like you here!"

I took the cigarettes and went out into the street. I opened the packet and lit one of them, and it tasted fine. They had cost me several shillings, but they always taste much better when you've won them off a machine.

There was a picture house just along the street, and I went in to waste a couple of hours. They were playing a film about a fellow who was always bottled, and who kicked his wife around all the time, and in the end she died, and he was so fed up about it that he shot himself. It didn't seem to make sense, because as far as he was concerned she had just been a bitch anyway, and he could have gone on drinking all the better without her clogging the place up. But a woman near me started sniveling away so loudly I had to move my seat, because the bitch in the film who died had a face that reminded me quite strongly of the kid, and it was annoying to have people sniveling at it, when they had probably never even seen her.

Just why my mind kept dropping back to her I couldn't make out. She was certainly so much less of a nuisance than the usual female that she stuck out a mile. But I didn't know her name, and I doubted whether I could find that house again in a hurry, and anyway I didn't go in for seeing the same woman twice.

When I came out of the picture house it was raining, so I ducked into a bar to get a drink. The barman was a nice friendly fellow, and the place wasn't busy yet. He started to talk, and I bought him a beer, because he was one of those fellows who talk and you don't seem to mind it much.

"I've heard of something for Saturday," he said.

"What's that?"

"There's a bloke comes in here," he said, "his brother-in-law's a jockey, and he says they've got it all set for this one."

I laughed and took a gulp of beer.

"I'll buy it," I said. "But judging by the number of fellows whose brothers-in-law are jockeys, these jockeys' mothers must breed like rabbits!"

The barman didn't seem to take to the joke, and he was a nice enough fellow, so I grinned and said, "Go on, cough it up!"

"Well, it's like this," he said. "This one's a three-year-old. It only raced twice as a two-year-old, and then it was shy of the gate, and it never did nothing. But now it's got over that, and they're going to spring it out sudden at a good price, see? Now when the weights come out for this race, this bloke's brother-in-law said to this bloke, now if they give him anything less than seven stone six, we just loose him off quietly and everything is all wrapped up, see?"

The barman paused.

"Hasn't the bloody thing got a name?" I asked him.

"That's just what I was coming to," he said. "As soon as the weights come out, this bloke comes rushing in here with the list and shows me, and I look down it, and what do I see but Petulant has been let in for seven stone!"

"I've never heard of the thing," I said.

"That's just it!" said the barman excitedly. "Nor has no one else!"

"Except every long-eared mug who comes in this pub," I said.

The barman looked very offended.

"All right, don't use it," he said. "But remember to watch out on Saturday, so as you can kick yourself for missing a ten to one."

I grinned at him. And then, suddenly, it went across my mind that he might be trying to play me. Having a dud horse tipped you so as a fellow can take a cushy bet is any mug's game. I put my hand tight round my glass.

"Can you get me a bet on it?" I asked.

I kept the grin on my face, but I was watching him closely. My hand was tight round my glass, ready to crash it up straight into his face if he said yes. But he shook his head.

"That's more than my license here is worth, old man," he said.

"Lucky for you," I said, and drank my beer; but he looked as if he didn't understand.

"I'll give it a try," I told him.

He moved off to serve another customer, and I picked up a paper that was lying on the bar and started to look through it casually. As I turned the first page, something caught my eye. For a minute I couldn't think what it was trying to say to me. *Your money does best at Benny's* and then there were pictures of hats and coats and a lot of other things.

I looked at it hard, and then I remembered where I had heard the name. "It's only half an hour from here," the kid had said, "and I get back at seven if I'm lucky."

I put down the paper and had another beer or two, and went across to the door to go out of the pub. As I got to the door I turned round and stood for a couple of seconds. Then I walked back to the bar, turned the paper over again, and tore out the bit about hats and coats. I put it in my pocket and went into the street.

Getting on for seven o'clock in the evening, I was fingering the bit of paper in my pocket and arguing the toss. There was no harm in being a sucker for once in a while. You could count on one hand the fellows who had done themselves any good with seeing the same woman twice, but what the hell? What had anyone else got to do with me? I pulled the bit of paper out of my pocket and looked at the address—17, 18, 19, and 20 Loumar Street.

I stopped a man in the street and asked him the way. Then I got a bus as he told me, and then got off and walked for a bit, and there it was sure enough. Benny seemed to be quite a fellow around there, with his name scrawled halfway down the street in lights.

I went inside, and the whole place was a seething mass of women. I backed out again quickly. You could hardly breathe in the place. I backed out and wandered around the building, wondering which way she would come out. The clock over the main doorway said twenty past six. From what she had said, they probably shut the place up and kicked the girls out at half-past.

Right round at the back there was a small door with a notice over it saying *Staff*. I took up a stand outside there and settled down to wait. I wondered what she would say at seeing me again. She night not take it very sweet. I couldn't quite make out why she had let me stick there that night anyway, and she might be sick of the sight of me now.

I moved back out of the light so that she shouldn't see me too soon. She might not want me hanging around. Nobody was going to tell me what to do and what not to do, but somehow or other the kid had to be given a chance to please herself a bit.

After about ten minutes of waiting, they came tumbling out in a heap. There were big ones and little ones, all muddled up together, and I tried to remember what size the kid was, and what she had been wearing. They were chattering away as hard as they could as they came down the steps, and then they were splitting up into twos and threes and scuttling off in all directions as fast as they could go.

Suddenly I saw her appear at the door and come down the steps. It was her all right, but she had got another one with her. They turned in the direction away from me, and started walking off together. I moved after them, wondering whether to cut in and tell the other one to clear off, but somehow or other I thought it might upset the kid, so I tagged along behind them for a bit to see what happened.

You can often get misunderstood for tagging along after a couple of people, but I kept looking around and nobody seemed to be taking any interest in me. After walking for a minute or two, they stopped on a corner and stood talking, and then the kid went on alone.

I caught her up and got in front of her and said, "Hullo!"

She looked a bit bewildered, and then she said, "Oh! You again!"

"Yes," I said. And then I wondered what to say next, because I hadn't come to tell her anything particular, and there didn't seem to be a lot of point in talking to her at all. But she eased me out by saying, "What do you want now?"

"I don't want anything, kid," I told her. "I've just come to say hullo."

"Hullo, then," she said, and went to move on.

"Wait a minute," I said, and started walking along beside her. I was wondering what was the way to play these parts. It's easy to handle them when they're being a nuisance, but what you do with them when they're no particular nuisance and there doesn't seem to be any point in talking to them anyway, takes a bit of getting used to.

We had only gone a few steps when she stopped again, and turned round and faced me.

"Let's get this straightened out," she said. "I don't run a hotel for lost sheep."

"That's all right, kid," I said. "I'm not looking for any hotel; I just came along to say hullo. There must be other people who've just come along to say hullo to people before."

She took the stiff look off her face a bit. "Well," she answered, "now that you've said hullo, what is supposed to happen next?"

She knew how to make it awkward all right. If it hadn't been her, I'd have smacked her face for talking at me. I began to wonder why the hell I had come.

"How are you doing?" I asked her.

She didn't answer.

"I didn't scare you the other night, did I?"

"Who, you?" she asked, and the talk dried up all over again.

We walked on a bit, and then she said, "Must you walk along beside me?"

"Listen, kid," I said. "I'm not trying to cut in on you, but I thought of going to the races on Saturday, and if you care to come along, I don't mind a bit."

"Really!" she said. "That's very nice of you, I'm sure, but as I shan't be coming, you won't have anything to mind about either way."

"You don't get me, kid," I said. "What I mean is that if you come along to the races with me, it'll be okay."

"That's all right," she said. "If I don't come it will be okay with me. Now do you mind leaving me?" She stopped, and we stood there for a minute looking at each other, and I felt like a mug.

"All right," I said.

She walked off quickly. I looked around, but no one seemed to be taking any notice of me, so I watched the kid walk down the road for a bit. And then I turned back and walked the other way, and ducked into a pub and had a few beers, and felt as if I'd like to slam somebody.

I stood by the bookies and watched them writ up the runners for the third race. So far, the day had done nothing to me at all. I hadn't brought my cards, or played any racket at all. I hadn't bet on the first two. I had simply wandered round like a mug, and I had been feeling like a mug, on and off, ever since speaking to the kid that evening.

But now they were writing up the runners for the third, and this was the race that the barman had been talking about. I couldn't go home just the same as I had come, so I thought I would have a look at the way they played Petulant, and see if there were any signs of anything. At first they were playing around three of them, and then one shortened and stood out clear at two to one. There wasn't even a price put up against Petulant. Then they brought him in at tens with a lot of others. He stuck around there for a bit, and there was nothing doing at all. Then, quite suddenly, it went nine, and then eight, and then seven. There was still a quarter of an hour to go, and I watched the lists all the time, but the three at the top were having it all their own way now, and nothing more was coming for Petulant. When the horses came out for the start, it was still at seven. It didn't smell bad to me.

I took out three pounds and gave them to the bookie. "Petulant," I said. Then I went and stood on the slope, but the crowd was thick and it meant straining your neck to see. The bell rang, and then everyone yelled and shouted. I lit a cigarette and waited for the numbers to go up in the frame. It was there all right. I collected my twenty-four quid.

This place was being nice. You couldn't have picked out a friendlier place if you tried. That barman was a good fellow. He would probably be as surprised as anyone, but he was a good fellow all the same. He was a good fellow by twenty-one quid, as far as I was concerned. I was feeling better now. I wasn't feeling such a mug anymore. You always feel your best when you've just got some money without even having to take it.

But after I got back to the town that night, I couldn't settle down. I went around the lighted streets and looked at the people, and watched the men and women going around together, and tried to talk myself out of it. I watched the men and the women walking arm in arm and talking to each other, and grinning at each other, and going all over the place together. They were just mugs. You could tell by the way they wandered around that they were just mugs. And yet they seemed to like it. Hell, yes, they seemed to like it.

I walked slowly back to the hotel and went to bed.

On the Wednesday night I tried her again. She was still showing how to make things awkward.

"Do I have to call a policeman?" she asked.

"What for? I'm only talking to you," I said.

"Exactly. But I don't want you to talk to me, and I don't want you to walk along with me either. If you insist, I shall have no alternative but to call a policeman. It would be rather an anticlimax, wouldn't it! Of course, while I am telling him that you won't leave me alone, I could also interest him with an account of how you forced your way into my room, and he might even be interested in knowing the part you played in that brawl in the public-house—"

"Shut up!" I told her. And then, in a quieter voice, I said, "You've got hold of the wrong end of the stick about that night."

"Indeed? I suppose you are going to tell me that I imagined it all!"

"No," I said, "but if you've been thinking all this time that I—"

"I assure you I haven't been thinking about you at all."

"Stuff up the clever talk," I told her. "Let's just get this one thing clear. I wasn't the fellow who slogged that poor chap in the pub. I was there, and I was mixed up in the general scrap, but it wasn't me who slogged him. The chap who did it bunked, and the rest of us lost our heads a bit and thought it wiser to clear off quick before we got caught up in trouble. I just happened to be the one they chose to chase. But I wasn't the one who slogged him. It wasn't me. Did those descriptions in the paper sound like me?"

I knew that last question was a winner. Those papers had been so confused about me that I had hardly recognized myself.

The kid was standing looking at me. I had said a piece, and I didn't know how it would go. We stood there, quiet, just looking at each other, and her eyes were trying to come inside me.

Suddenly she spoke.

"Shall I tell you something peculiar?"

"What?"

"I'd like to believe that. I'd like to very much."

And before I had sorted it out and made any meaning of it at all, she was right down the street and around the corner and out of sight.

Three nights running now I had walked right back to her front door with her, and she didn't seem to mind. And I didn't seem to mind either. Somehow the feeling of mug-with-a-woman soon left you, when it was her. It seemed a bit silly for her to go inside and for me to wander off again to wait for the next evening, so I asked her what about coming out and eating with me somewhere. She said she didn't mind, and we wandered off to a place I had been to before, where they put you up a nice meal.

We sat down at a table and I looked around, but at most of the tables there were pairs of people, a lot of them mugs with women, and nobody seemed to be taking much notice of me, so I felt all right.

The waiter gave her a menu and she ordered some fried fish, but I took the menu out of her hand and looked at it, and told the waiter to bring chicken, and to make it big helpings.

"Let's celebrate," I explained.

"What are we celebrating?" she asked.

"We're celebrating that you're not turning your back on me any longer," I told her, "and that I don't feel a mug hanging around you anymore."

She laughed.

"You've got a funny way of putting things," she said. "What's your name, anyway?"

"Use Bill," I told her.

"Is that all there is?"

"There's a Saunders after it."

"And who are you?" she asked.

"I've just told you," I said.

"I mean, what do you do?"

"I just get around," I said.

"Get around where?"

"Different places."

"Doing what?"

"Different things," I said. "What about you?"

"You know all there is to know about me," she said. "I spend my young life telling unattractive women how charming they look in Benny's hats. But you haven't told me what your job is yet."

"I've told you I just get around."

"But how do you earn your living?" she asked.

"Any way that happens," I said, and grinned at her. But she didn't seem to get it.

"I believe you're ashamed of your job," she laughed.

The waiter brought the chicken and we tucked in, and didn't talk anymore until we had finished it. Then I told the waiter to bring some apple pie and cream, and then we had some coffee. I gave her a cigarette, and when I had lit it she took it out of her mouth and the lipstick showed all red on it.

"You certainly keep yourself dolled up!" I told her.

She laughed.

"You wouldn't like me plain and unadorned," she said. "You wait until you see me first thing in the morning."

"You've got a rotten memory," I told her, and she laughed again.

The place had been pretty full when we came in, but it was getting emptier now. We lingered over our cups until she said it was time to go, because she was tired and wanted to get to bed.

"Have we been here that long?" I asked.

It was funny how the time slipped by with her. She was nice to look at, and she seemed to think a lot of things were funny, and she was altogether a change from the sours you usually knock up against.

I paid the bill, and we got up and walked back together to her front door.

"Good night," she said. "And thanks for the meal."

"There's some more races on Saturday," I told her.

"I hope you enjoy them," she laughed. "Good night!" And she went in and shut the door behind her.

Chapter Four: THE THREE-CARD TRICK

They are putting up the names for the second race when we get there. It is getting on for three o'clock by that time, because the kid doesn't leave the shop until one o'clock on Saturdays, and apart from that, there was still quite a bit of persuading left over from the night before. But the sun was shining, and the town was looking a stuffy kind of place, and the race course sounded nicer than the streets, and with one thing and another I managed to talk her into it.

As soon as the kid has made up her mind to do anything, she goes right at it. One minute she wasn't coming for anything in the world, and the very next minute the great big worry was how many races we should miss.

Well, they are putting up the names for the second as we get there, and from what I can see it's a bookie's race, with nothing sticking out by an inch, but the kid sees it differently. From the way she is going on you'd think it was the Derby at least.

"Bunny Boy!" she exclaims, and grabs my jacket and tugs it. "What a lovely name! Let's bet on Bunny Boy. I know he'll win."

"He's never done it yet," I tell her.

"Never mind that," she says, "he sounds just sweet. Look, that man there with a bowler hat just whispered something to the bookie, and they rubbed the numbers out. What does that mean? Look, his friend is looking through the binoculars at something on the top of the grandstand. It's that man up there, and he's signaling something! Oh! Isn't it exciting! Look, Bill, they are chalking up the numbers again. That five means that Bunny Boy is five to one, doesn't it? Oh! I must back it!"

If the kid can see something in the play that I'm missing, then it's okay with me. I pull out a pound to give to her.

"Here, put this on for yourself," I tell her. She looks at it and gasps.

"What—a pound?" she exclaims. "You must be mad. Anyhow, I couldn't take it from you, and I wouldn't dream of putting more than a shilling on— I wouldn't dare, I should be terrified."

I look at her hard for a second, but she doesn't seem to be poking me. She is much too excited for that. I look down and find myself holding the pound note in my hand like a fool, so I shove it back in my pocket. Then she opens her handbag and gets out a shilling and goes over to the bookie. "A shilling on Bunny Boy, please."

"Seven bob to one Bunny Boy ticket number eighty-seven thank you lady!"

She comes running back with the ticket in her hand.

"He talked so quickly I could hardly make out what he said, but I think it's all right," she says. "Do they start soon?"

"Pretty soon," I tell her.

"Let's go up the top there, and we'll be able to see better."

Up we go to the top of the public stand, me edging a few mugs out of the way to make room for her. The horses aren't out yet, but they soon come frisking along for the start, and she grabs my jacket again and pulls it so hard I have to tell her not to tear it.

"Which one is it?" she asks.

"Number seven," I tell her.

"Oh, he's not here," she says desperately. "Where has he got to? Oh, there he is! Yes, look! Number seven, the blue jockey with the pink cap. Isn't he marvelous? I know he's going to beat them all. Isn't he much the nicest-looking horse of the lot? Don't you wish you'd backed him too?"

The kid stood to win seven shillings, and I hadn't bet myself, but that didn't seem to be making any difference. She is so worked up about the thing that I begin to think that maybe, somehow or other, there is going to be some kick in this race after all. With her getting so cooked up, I begin to pick up a bit of the backwash.

"He certainly looks in nice condition, kid."

They line up at the starting gate in front of the stand, and the kid is so much on her toes by now that I am getting ready to hold her back from jumping down there and running out to give Bunny Boy a smack on the rump. Then the gate goes flying up, and the kid's panting disappears in the sudden roar that flashes through the crowd.

The field goes off in a bunch, and you can't pick out anything particular. They go easy up to the fork and disappear, and the place quiets down except for a few silly mugs who are explaining to their friends that so-and-so is having it all his own way.

Then suddenly another roar goes up, and it means that someone has spotted them coming back into the straight. The kid starts jumping up and down, and straining for all she's worth.

"There they are! Is it him? Where is he? Oh—where's Bunny Boy?"

"Blackie's in the lead," says a fellow next door to us. "Blackie's there. Blackie's got it easily."

"Oh, come on, Bunny Boy! Where's Bunny Boy?"

"It's early yet," I tell her, rescuing a button that she looks like dragging clean off my jacket. "It's the last two hundred yards that does it on this course."

They are coming along well into view now, and I can pick out Bunny Boy lying fourth. I point him out to the kid. She starts to scream her head off as the horse begins to move up.

"Come on, Bunny Boy!" a voice bellows, and I start to feel a bit of a mug when I realize it's my voice. The kid's excitement has got right into me. They come along riding a fine finish, and we both bellow "Bunny Boy!" until we've got no more wind.

"Oh, isn't he marvelous!" she says. "I knew he'd do it. I knew all the time he'd do it!"

"I'm not sure he did," I answer. "I think he was just pipped."

"Oh, don't be ridiculous," she says. "Come on, I'm going to get my money."

Before I can stop her she is off down the steps of the stand, and oozing quickly through the crowd toward the bookies. Before I can get to the slates she is back looking for me. Her face is popping with excitement.

"They don't know yet," she says. "They don't know yet who's won."

"You've got to wait for the flag," I tell her. "Look, see where that tall frame is? They'll put the numbers up in there, and then you've got to wait for the flag."

As I'm saying this, up goes the seven in the frame.

"Looks like you're okay, kid." And sure enough, up goes the weigh-in flag.

"Now collect," I tell her.

She struggles up to the bookie again, waving her ticket importantly, and comes back looking as if she has won the world.

"Aren't I lucky?" she exclaims. "And I picked him out all by myself, didn't I?"

She grabs my arm and drags me off to look at everything and everybody. She picks you up like booze, does the kid when she is like this. But the other three races each take a shilling from her, and in the last race the horse she picks is so far behind that even she can't get up very much excitement. So we're a bit quieter as we shuffle with the crowd away from the course. But she's looking as pleased as anything still, and she fishes out four shillings and waves them in my face.

"I'm still that up," she says.

"That's a fine afternoon's work," I agree. "Now what about some tea?"

"Yes, out of the winnings!" she exclaims, with a seriousness that makes me laugh.

"I've got a bit more than that," I tell her, but she starts to insist.

"Really," she says, "I want to. You brought me here, and now I've won this money, and I'm going to take you out to tea."

As we move off to look for a tea-place, I scratch my mind to try to remember when anyone ever wanted to take me out to tea before, and I begin to wonder if I can really make head or tail of it all.

But it doesn't much matter. When the races can start to be fun like this, just because the kid is all warmed up and panting about it, then it doesn't much matter.

We sat over tea until the tea was cold and it was getting dusk outside.

"I'm worn out with excitement," she said.

I looked at her and wondered what it was. It was difficult to put your finger on the difference. But if you wanted it tough, you came to the races, and now the races were turned into a playground because the kid was there.

"Bill," she said suddenly, "why did you bring me here?"

"I don't know," I said. It seemed a silly question. "I just wanted to, I suppose."

"Do you come to the races often?"

"Often enough."

"Do you always bring a girl with you?"

"This is the first time," I said.

She laughed.

"Don't lay it on too thick," she said.

"This is the first time," I told her, but she laughed again. Then she asked:

"What do you do for a living?"

"Different things," I said.

"Such as what?"

I never tried to explain anything like that before.

"I do all sorts of different things," I explained.

"Tell me one of them, for instance."

I was stuck for this a bit. You could tell most people anything you wanted, and they could like it or not. But with the kid you needed to keep up a bit of a show.

I turned my mind over, and thought that perhaps I could hedge her off with the cards. I pulled them out of my pocket.

"Here's one thing," I said. "Have you seen this one?"

"What is it?"

I showed her the three cards. "You've got to pick out the lady," I explained.

"Is that what they call the three-card trick?" she asked.

"That's right," I said.

"I thought that was cheating."

I laughed. "Not the way I do it," I told her. "I do it fair and square. I show you the three cards face upward, like this, and then I turn them down on the table, and you have to pick up the lady if you can."

"It sounds easy enough," she said. "I've never seen it before, but I've always heard of it as if there were some trick in it that didn't give the other person a chance."

"It's got a bad name," I explained to her, "because of the way people play it. You can find people playing it in race trains, and on the course itself if you look around. They do it with two or three fellows. They get hold of a mug, and let him win once or twice when there is no money on it, and then as soon as he puts money on, if he wins, they make him go on until he loses."

"But what if he just walks away when he has won?" she asked.

"That's the point," I explained. "There are always two or three fellows playing it together. They crowd round the mug, and if he tries to get away with the money, that's just bad luck for him."

"You mean it's done with a kind of gang?"

"That's right. That's the dirty way they do it. They crowd up on the fellow, about four to one, and he hasn't got a chance. But I do it alone. That's fair enough, isn't it?"

She laughed. "It sounds all right, but where's the catch?"

"Have a go," I suggested, and showed her the three cards, face up. "Keep your eye on the lady."

I took the three cards in my hands, two in one hand and one in the other. Then I threw them face down on the table, side by side.

"Which is it?" I asked her.

She pointed. "That one," she said.

It was two to one against her, and she was wrong. The three cards were lying face down on the table, and I turned up the queen, which wasn't the one she had pointed to.

"You're wrong," I said, showing her. "Now watch closely again."

I picked the three cards up again, and did the same thing as before. This time she pointed straight to the queen.

"Got it," I said, and turned up the one she had pointed to. "Now try again."

We went through the whole thing a third time, and she picked out the queen again, without hesitating.

"See the idea?" I asked her.

She was laughing.

"Bill," she said, "you'll never win any money if you do it like that. Why—the corner of the queen is turned up a tiny bit, and I can tell it every time from the back."

"Bright girl!" I said. "Now just pretend you're having a pound on it."

I picked up the cards again, showed them to her carefully, and threw them face down on the table.

"Now suppose you're having a pound on it," I said.

"I should hate to take your money," she laughed, "but that's the one."

I turned up the card she pointed to. It wasn't the queen. I grinned at her, and the way her face fell was a treat.

"But, Bill," she exclaimed, "I could have sworn that the card which was slightly bent up at one corner was the queen. It was, the last two times."

"You're beginning to get it," I said. "The corner of the queen is turned up slightly while we have the first few trial goes. Then you get to thinking that you can tell the queen from the back, and so when you put your money on it, you pick out the card with the corner turned slightly up. But as soon as you've got money on it, the one with the corner turned up isn't the queen, it's one of the others."

"But, Bill—" She looked puzzled, just the way they always do.

"Try it again, Bill," she said, perking up as if she really knew better than me, and had simply made a mistake for once.

I picked the cards up, and showed them to her, and threw them down again. This time I turned the corner up rather more than before, and she looked up and laughed.

"I wasn't quite sure before," she said, "but thanks for telling me. That's the one." She deliberately avoided the one with the corner turned up, and went for one of the others.

"Wrong again," I said, and I turned over the one with the corner flipped up, and showed her that it was the queen.

"As soon as you tumble to the trick," I explained, "then the queen starts to turn up her corner again, just to fool you."

She laughed. "Is that all there is in it?" she asked.

"It's not such a little," I said. "I took a lot of trouble practicing that. You see, I told you the point, and that quickened things up for you. But suppose I am playing it with a stranger! I've got to watch him closely, and see when he tumbles to it, so that I can decide when to change the turned-up corner. As I throw the cards down the first time the man thinks he can follow which it is. Then he finds he's wrong, so then he looks at the one he thinks ought to be the queen, and decides there must be some quick-handed trick about it, and that it must be one of the other two instead. Then, after two or three tries, he starts to notice the turned-up corner, and watches for it. When he points to the wrong card, you don't turn up that card to show him he is wrong, but you turn up the queen, wherever it is, so as gradually to lead his attention to the fact that it's got a turned-up corner. As soon as you gather he has tumbled to the turned-up corner, then, as you pick the three cards up, you turn up the corner of one of the others instead."

She gaped at me as if I were a magician.

"Well!" she said. "If someone invites me to do it I shall know what to do, and I shall make my fortune out of them."

I frowned at her. "Don't ever let me catch you playing it," I told her. "It's a mug's game for anyone except the man who holds the cards, especially with the kind of mobs who usually run it. Don't ever fall into it, kid."

"Don't you ever lose at it?" she asked.

"Lose at it? Why should I lose at it? If the fellow gets too fly for me I just—" I hesitated.

"You just what?"

"I just go on playing until I win," I said quickly. And before she could start to get a nuisance with her questions, I thumped the table and beckoned the waitress across and asked her how much for the tea. I paid the bill, making the kid put her money back into her purse.

"Come on," I said, "we had better get the train back home."

We went out of the tea-shop and walked along the road for about half a mile until we came to the station. The crowds had all cleared off by now, and there were only a few people waiting about on the platform for the train. It looked like a perfect situation with plenty of choice. It looked as if there would be a dozen carriages to choose from, with only a person or two in each.

I looked down at the kid. It would be a pity for her to get ideas into her head that she might not like, but at the same time I couldn't tag along with her forever and let everything slide.

The train came in, and a fellow who looked like a pretty good mug got into an empty carriage.

"Come on," I said to her, and caught her by the arm and made to go in after him.

She tugged me back quickly.

"This is a first-class carriage, Bill," she said.

"Come on," I said; "we'll pay the difference. It looks pretty cozy in here."

She climbed in, looking questions at me. I grinned.

"Been a pretty nice day, hasn't it?"

"Lovely," she answered.

The train started to move out of the station. I guessed it would take about three-quarters of an hour. I could take my time. There wasn't any hurry.

I snuggled into a corner of the carriage, with the kid opposite me. She looked very tired, and after a minute or two she shut her eyes. I glanced at the fellow in the far corner. He looked a mug all right.

I lit a cigarette, and then asked him casually, "Been to the races?"

"Yes," he said. "Have you?"

The kid wasn't taking any notice. She must have dropped asleep. She looked tired out.

"Yes," I said. "It's a fairly new experience for me. I don't often go to race meetings. Did you do any good?"

He nodded. "Yes, I did," he admitted. "I backed three winners, and finished the day well up."

This was a mug all right. This was a mug who advertised the fact. I shot another look at the kid; but she was asleep sure enough. I pulled my three cards out.

"I've had a pretty bad day," I told the mug. "I got watching a fellow doing the three-card trick, and I couldn't resist having a bet or two, but he was too clever for me. So in the end I asked him if he would sell me his three cards, because I felt so sure that there must be a trick about them. But I was wasting my money. They are just plain cards."

I handed them across to him. He looked at them with interest.

"Really!" he exclaimed. "I've often wondered about that myself. Yes, they look quite ordinary. Are you sure these are the ones he did the trick with?"

"Pretty well positive. It must be the way they throw them down or something."

I picked them up in my hands and threw them down together on the seat. Then I picked up one of them myself and looked at it. I laughed.

"I can fool myself all right," I said to him.

He laughed.

I picked them up and threw them down again. He nodded to the end one. I picked it up and showed him. It was the queen.

"It wouldn't do for me to do it!" I said.

I picked them up and threw them down once or twice, pretending to be puzzling the thing out.

After a bit I said, "I think I've got it. See if you can follow it."

I did it twice, with him guessing, and he got it wrong once and right once.

I grinned at him. "Let's do it in style," I said, and pulled out a pound note and put it on the seat.

The mug hesitated, then he said, "All right, but I warn you I have got pretty good eyesight for this kind of thing."

I showed him the cards, then threw them down, and he guessed the one in the middle.

I pointed to the right-hand one. "I think it's this one," I said, and turned it up. It was the queen. I collected his pound and left it on the seat with mine. Then I picked up the cards again.

"Bad luck," I said. "Double or quits?"

"All right—just once," he said.

I threw the cards down, and watched his face carefully. The queen had had the corner turned up the time before, and I'd got it turned up again this time, and I thought I saw his eyes fasten on it. Sure enough he pointed to the one with the corner up. I handed him back his pound.

I picked up the cards again, and threw them down again. He pretended to be puzzled, then he pointed to the one with the corner turned up. But I had fooled him on it, and as he passed his pound back again, his puzzled look was a real one.

I went through the thing again, and he was wrong again. I'd got him on the run now, because he was avoiding the one with the corner turned up, and that was queen again now. But he wasn't such a mug as I thought. Suddenly he pointed to the queen. Then he got it right twice more running. He was picking on pure chance, and the luck was running with him. He was four pounds up, and he suddenly sat back and said:

"That's enough. I don't want to go on taking your money."

"Go on," I said. "You haven't finished yet."

"No, really," he protested, "I feel that I'm in luck, and I know that if we go on I shall only win more and more. I think we had better stop."

"Go on," I told him. "Put your money down on the seat and we'll play for it."

He frowned.

"What do you mean?" he asked. "I'm perfectly entitled to stop playing if I want to."

The kid was still asleep. The train was beginning to run into the outskirts of the town. I had not reckoned on it working out like this. I must have been bungling my cards pretty badly. Anyway, there wasn't much time left now, and I should have to deal with this mug, because he seemed to think he could sit on the money.

"Bring it out," I told him.

"I shall do nothing of the kind," he said.

There wasn't much time. I hadn't got time to argue with him. I moved across beside him and cracked my fist into his eye. He slabbed over backward as if the end of the world had come. He put his hands up to protect his face, but he didn't try to hit back.

"Cough it up," I said. "Mine, and yours too."

I put my hands toward the pocket where he'd put the money. He put down his hands to stop me. The back yards of the houses were on both sides of the train by now. It would be slowing up soon.

I pulled back my arm, and let him have it hard. As he crumpled up on the seat there was a scream behind me. I spun round, and there was the kid awake, with a horrified stare on her face.

"What are you doing?" she gasped.

I turned away from her. There wasn't any time to talk about it now. I put my hand into his pocket and pulled out the money.

"Bill!" she screamed. "No, Bill!"

I turned round toward her, but she cringed away from me. Then, before I could guess what she was going to do, she suddenly put up her hand and pulled the communication cord. I grabbed her arm, but it was too late. I felt the train check speed. I threw her back onto the seat and for two pins I'd have smashed her up.

"You interfering bitch!" I said.

She didn't answer. She just looked at me as if she would like to spit at me. If it hadn't been her, I'd have kicked her in the guts.

The brakes were grinding hard, and the train was just on stopping. I got hold of her wrist tightly, and with my other hand I opened the carriage door. The door handle was toward the front of the train, so that as soon as the catch was undone, the weight of the door swung it back and wide open.

For a moment she struggled to get free. Then when she looked round again at the man on the seat, a kind of panic seemed to get hold of her. She stopped struggling, and stood quite limp.

"We must get out of this," I said quickly.

We could have lodged the mug in the corner and disappeared easily enough at the station, but now that she had pulled the alarm cord, they would be along looking for trouble, and there wouldn't be much chance of covering up.

Just as the train was squealing to a standstill, I got hold of her with both hands and planted her on the edge by the open door. It was dark and black down there in the drop toward the ground, but the lights were just reflecting on the other rails, and it was easy enough to gauge the distance.

"Don't wait until it stops. Jump now. Try to land on all fours, and jump as hard as you can or the door may catch you."

The train was just stopping as she jumped. I saw her land on her hands and knees, and I jumped after her. But the jolt of the train being brought to a standstill jerked the door forward, and as I sprang, I caught my head on the edge of it, and I spun round in the air and landed on my back. For a moment I lay there dazed, but only for a moment. Doors were opening, windows were dropping down, and heads were popping out all along the train.

I pulled myself together and looked round for the kid. She was standing a few yards away from me, gaping round as if she didn't know what to do. I dived for her and grabbed her arm.

"Come on, quick!" I said.

As we made off across the rails, the lights from the carriage windows picked us out a bit, and we heard some shouts from behind us. The guard was coming along the train, and he spotted us running and started to chase us. Pulling the kid behind me, I ran as fast as I could tug her, taking a slanting direction and gradually bearing across the four or five pairs of rails toward the edge of the track.

We came to the top of a sudden slope, where the ground was banked up for the rails.

"Jump!" I shouted, as I saw the signal wires just in time.

We scrambled down the slope and came to a fence. It was a wooden fence about four feet high. I looked quickly both ways, but I couldn't see an opening in it. It was the common back fence of a lot of thin slips of backyards, behind a row of slum houses, all built in a long solid block that looked as if it didn't end anywhere.

I pulled the kid up suddenly.

"Be quiet," I said softly. We stood in the darkness and listened. I could hear a few shouts going on, but they were in the distance now. Down at the bottom of the slope we were out of sight of the train. I put my hand up and felt the top of the fence, to make sure there was no glass or barbed wire.

"Over you go!" I said.

I lifted her up and sat her on the top of the fence, and then lifted her legs up and pushed them over, and gave her a little shove and she plopped down on the other side. Then I pulled myself up by my hands and scrambled over after her.

We were in the backyard of one of the houses now. But the houses being built tight up against each other, with no gaps between them anywhere, the only ways out of the backyard were the way we had come, or over the side fences into other backyards, or through the house.

There was a light showing through the back door. I got hold of the kid's arm again and pulled her toward the house.

"Just stick close behind me," I told her, "and keep your mouth shut."

I tried the handle of the door, but it was locked. So I knocked hard on the glass at the top half of it.

Presently a kid's voice came from inside, "There's someone knocking on the back door, Ma!"

"Stop your nonsense," said a woman's voice "You're always imagining things."

"But there is, Ma—I heard it," said the first voice again, and into the half-lighted passage a boy kid came. He looked through the glass, but the glimmering light was behind him and he couldn't see through it.

He unlocked the door and opened it, and peered out. I kicked the door out of his hand and walked in past him, dragging the kid behind me.

"Who are you?" asked the boy, and then in a shout, "Ma, there's a man and a girl come into the house!"

We walked straight through a passage, which led right through the house from back to front. But before we could get to the front door, a woman came out of a room on the side.

"Here, who are you and what do you think you're doing?" she asked, and put herself right in the way.

She had got plenty of size all right. She plugged the passage.

"Out of the way," I told her.

"Out of the way!" she spluttered. "What do you think you're doing, breaking in and ordering me about in my own house?"

She was the kind that argues forever. She was standing right outside of the door she had come through. I took hold of her arm and turned her round slightly so that she was backing the door. Then I gave her a good prod in the belly, and she squelched and sagged back into the room and sat down hard on her bottom.

I grabbed the kid again and made for the front door. We went through it and slammed it behind us. There wasn't anyone about in the street.

"Come," I said, still lugging the kid. We made off along the street as fast as she could keep up. I heard the boy screaming from the house, but it died away as we ran, and nobody followed us up. When we got a few streets away, I pulled up to give the kid a rest, for she was panting hard by now.

As we stopped, she jerked her arm out of my hand, and stood there gasping for a moment or two.

"As soon as you've got your breath we'll get going again," I said. "We'd better not hang around."

She was breathing easier now. I took hold of her arm to move off again, but she snatched it away.

"Wait a minute," she said. "Do you think I'm coming with you?"

"Don't start any argument," I told her. "You've been enough nuisance for one night."

I put my hand out to take hold of her, but she backed quickly away. Then she suddenly burst out in a fierce, hating voice:

"You've been enough forever!"

"What the—"

I felt the sting of her hand on my face, and I put up my hands instinctively. But there wasn't any scrap. She had turned on her heel and was off already, walking quickly down the street. I opened my mouth to call after her, but the words dried up on me. I felt the sting of her hand on my face as I watched her get farther and farther down the street. When somebody hits you it warms you up. When a mug lands back at you, it gets you going. But somehow or other I wasn't warmed up now. I stood there and watched the back of her, walking quickly away out of sight, until all I could see in the dark was the vague lightness of her legs. Then she turned at the end of the street and was gone round the corner.

I stood there for quite a few minutes, looking along the empty street. Then I shrugged my shoulders and lit a cigarette, and dusted down my clothes from the scramble. As I walked off slowly, to find my way back, I could still feel the sting of her hand on my face.

Chapter Five: A BLOODY JAM

"I can't pretend that I didn't know you were a tough guy. I was fool enough to allow myself to be attracted by that. But I thought there was something decent underneath. Now I know there isn't. You're nothing but a cheap, bullying hooligan."

It hangs around as if she'd said it yesterday, instead of three weeks ago. It hangs around and gets inside of me and I can't shake it off.

She doesn't understand that there was one of me and one of him, and that it wasn't my fault that he hadn't any guts. She doesn't understand that I didn't mean to hit him at all, and that it only turned out that I had to because I bungled the cards. She doesn't understand that I thought she was too fast asleep to wake up then, and that if she had stayed asleep a bit longer I could have shot her out quick at the station without her seeing anything.

But she doesn't *want* to understand.

She's looking up with her eyes stone cold, and turning away and refusing to talk.

She's coming up with a girlfriend on either side, and deliberately getting them to walk with her all the way home.

She's giving me the slip by dodging out of the customers' entrance, with me standing there waiting by the back entrance until they shut it up.

To hell with her. "Give me another beer, miss!"

No woman's going to make a mug out of me. No woman's going to have me mooning around over her. No woman's going to have me minding what she thinks, about me or anything else.

"Give me another beer, Curly!"

"Who d'you think you're calling Curly?"

"Give me another beer!"

The damned streets. You get sick of wandering round the streets, looking at men with women of their arms. The whole place seems to be cluttered up with men with women hanging on their arms.

Slab-faced bitches they are, too. Only a mug would hang any woman on his arm.

So you want the soft play, do you? You want to get yourself a nice sweet sucker, eh?

"Give me another beer!"

The room was littered with screwed-up balls of paper by the time I had finished writing. It wouldn't look right, written down. It would sound all right if you said it, but it seemed to go flat when it was written down. And yet there wasn't any other way. Hanging around trying to talk to her didn't look like getting me anywhere. I couldn't see how to force her to talk, without getting tough, and this thing had to be handled the dandy way.

At last I got it good, and folded the paper carefully and put it into an envelope. But when I had stuck the envelope down, I suddenly realized that I couldn't address it because I didn't know what her name was. I had never asked her. There had seemed no particular reason for wanting to know it. But I couldn't post a letter without a name on it.

I tucked it in my pocket and went along to Benny's in good time that evening. In the street nearby I collared a kid who was idling about, and asked him if he wanted to earn a shilling.

"You betcha, mister," he said. "What do I have to do for it?"

"You just wait until a girl comes along, and then you give her this letter," I said.

"Any girl?" he asked.

"I'll show you when she comes," I told him. "Come on up the street here, because I don't want her to see me. When I point her out to you, then you take this letter and give it to her, and don't say where you got it."

I took him up the street away from Benny's, in the direction the kid would come. Then I hid in a doorway, with the boy beside me, and waited for her to show up.

"I write letters to a girl," said the boy.

"Shut up," I said.

"All right, I'll shut up. But I do write them just the same."

Just then I saw the kid coming along with another girl.

"There she is," I said to the boy. "Now take it over and give it to her and don't say anything. Then scuttle off and make yourself scarce until she's gone. I'll be waiting here. When she's gone out of sight, come back to me and I'll give you the shilling."

The boy took the letter.

"There's two of 'em," he said. "Does it matter which one I give it to?"

"The one on the inside," I said.

"All right, mister; I think you're right. She's the best one." And he hurried off toward them.

From the doorway I watched him get up to the kid and hand her the letter. She took it, looked at the envelope, and looked back as if to question him. But the boy had scuttled off down the street the way I had told him. She looked after him, looked at the envelope again, and then the two of them examined it together.

Then the kid started to open it. She moved along until she was under a street light, and pulled out the paper from inside and started to read it. The other girl was looking at it with her, but as soon as they started to read, the kid moved it away so that the other girl couldn't see it.

Then she screwed it up quickly and it looked as if she was going to throw it away. But she hesitated, and looked up and down the street as if she was expecting to see someone. Then she opened her handbag, stuffed in the crumpled bit of paper, said something to her friend, and they both walked on.

As soon as she was out of sight, the boy came running back to where I was standing. He held out his hand and I gave him a shilling.

"Thanks, mister," he said.

He was just going off with it, when he looked round at me and said with a very serious face, "She's nicer than mine, mister."

Then he turned to go, but I called him back.

"Here," I said, and gave him another shilling.

He looked at me for a moment as if he thought I'd gone funny. Then he went hurtling down the street before I'd have a chance to take it back again.

"Have another drink," I said.

He'd had four or five. It was taking him a long time to find his guts.

"I could use the money," he said, "but I don't want to get into no trouble."

"There isn't going to be any," I said. "You can run, can't you? When anything like that happens, the crowd always gapes round the girl until you're clear away."

"Supposing there's a cop near?"

"We can pick a time when there isn't. Don't make it all sound so difficult."

"You won't slog me too hard, will you?" he asked.

I shook my head. "Don't worry," I said. "If I put you out so that you can't beat it quickly, then we'll both get caught up in a lot of questions. And that isn't what I want at all. Don't worry—it'll be just a gentle tap."

He poured some more beer down him.

"They can put you in jug for it," he said.

"They don't put anyone in jug unless they catch them," I said. "What do you want me to do? Give you the dough for going up and kissing her?"

I pulled a pound note from my pocket and twiddled it in my fingers while he watched it.

"I could do with the dough," he said again.

I was getting sick of this.

"It's the easiest money anyone ever earned," I said. "If you don't want it, somebody else will."

I put the note back in my pocket and got up. He was on his feet immediately.

"I'll do it, mister," he said, and held out his hand eagerly. There was a greedy look in his eye.

I gave him the money.

"Come on," I said.

We went outside and started to walk quickly. After about fifteen minutes we got to the corner. I pulled him up.

"Listen," I said. "If you muck this and try to give me the slip, I'll catch you up and slam you to pieces. Now, go down there and wait just past that pillar-box."

I watched him slink along the pavement. When he got to the pillar-box he stopped, and propped himself up against the wall.

A clock was striking seven. There shouldn't be long to wait.

She came out pretty punctually. I said, "Hullo," and she turned her head away and walked straight on. We were getting to do it like an act, as if we had practiced it up together and knew just how it went.

I watched her walk along the pavement toward the pillar-box. I went slowly along after her, keeping a distance of about thirty yards between us. I could see the fellow still lounging there, looking at me, and I put up my hand and scratched my head in the way I had told him to look for, to show him when it was her.

As the kid drew level with him he sudden came to life and made for her and grabbed her bag. At the same instant I started to run forward as fast as I could. It only took me a few seconds to come up to them. They were doing a feeble struggle, both clutching the handbag.

"You dirty swine!" I said, getting hold of him and swinging him away from her, and giving him smack on the face.

A couple of people from the other side of the street were running over. As soon as I had smacked him, the fellow took to his heels and shot round the corner like a rabbit. Sure enough, nobody went after him. Two fellows who had come across the street raised their hats and asked if she was all right. She said she was. It was pretty easy to see that she was. They raised their hats again, and moved off. I began to feel that the thing had looked a bit tame.

The kid turned round to me.

"That was very gallant of you," she said. "But you are losing your touch. I seem to remember that you used to be able to hit people considerably harder than that. When you see your friend again, please thank him for attacking me so gently."

Then she turned round and walked away stiffly, in the way she was getting so good at. I stumped off the opposite way, like anybody's mug.

I had talked her into letting me stay in her room that first night. I had talked her into coming to the races. She was clearly a girl you could talk into things, if only you could get hold of her to talk to. But you couldn't talk to anyone who just turned her back on you and walked away. If only there was some place I could get her, where she couldn't turn her back and walk away—

I pulled myself up suddenly, and wondered why I hadn't thought of it before. She would turn her back on me, would she? She would walk away and refuse to talk, would she? Oh no, she wouldn't do anything of the kind.

The next morning I walked into Benny's.

A man who looked as if he were just ready to bury somebody came forward. "Can I assist you, sir?"

"Beat it," I told him.

He raised his eyebrows. "I beg your pardon, sir?"

"All right," I said, "I'm just looking around."

"Certainly, sir," he said, and looked at me as if he knew for sure that I was trying to pinch something.

I started to wander round the place. It seemed to stretch on forever. There were hundreds of women selling things and buying things, but I couldn't see the kid. I walked all round the ground floor, and then went upstairs, and then again up more stairs, through masses of corsets and underclothes and ribbons, and women all the time. But I couldn't see the kid. I was just beginning to think I had drawn a blank, and just going to get out before I was suffocated, when I saw her walk along and plonk a hatbox down on a counter. I walked quickly over to her.

"Hullo!" I said.

She looked up. I had never seen her look quite so furious.

"What are you doing here?" she asked.

"I've just come to talk to you," I said.

"You can't talk to me here," she said quickly. "Go away! You'll make me lose my job."

"This is just the place I can talk to you," I said.

"Go away! Please, go away!" she exclaimed. "I shall get into trouble if I'm seen just talking to you."

I grinned. "I'll go away if you'll promise to meet me tonight," I said.

"Certainly not!" she said, and looked down and fumbled about with the hatbox.

"Then I'll stay here until you talk to me," I said.

She looked up again, not so much furious now as scared. A woman who looked like some kind of a superintendent was standing farther along the counter and beginning to take a lot of interest in us. "All right," the kid said quickly; "I'll meet you outside tonight, but please go away now."

I walked away and made for the door, and was glad to get out of the place. The man in the black suit bowed as I got to the door, and it was hard to walk past him. If he had known what saved him from having his face smashed in, he would have given the kid a rise in salary.

She kept her word. I was waiting outside the store when she came out, and she came out alone and walked straight up to where I was standing, and stopped in front of me.

"Well?" she asked.

"Let's walk along," I said. Her voice wasn't too friendly. She had kept her word, but all the same her voice wasn't very promising.

We walked along, while I tried to think up something to say. She didn't seem as if she wanted to help me out.

"You don't seem to have much to talk about," I said.

"I? There's nothing I want to talk about. I thought it was you who wanted to talk," she said.

"So I do," I answered. "But I just want to talk the way we used to talk—not about anything special, but just talking."

In a stony-cold voice she said, "There's nothing I want to talk to you about. I have no wish to talk to you at all. I'm only talking to you now because you took a mean advantage of me in the shop today and forced me to. I might have expected something like that of you. There's nothing a man like you wouldn't stoop to!"

"What do you mean?" I asked her. "If I want to get you to talk to me, don't I have to think up a way? Is a fellow to give up just because someone says they won't talk to him? Don't I have to find a way? Can anyone get along at all without finding a way?"

She stopped and faced me. I stopped as well, and we stood there in the street looking at each other. Her face was hard, without any friendliness at all.

"You needn't trouble to find a way where I'm concerned," she said. "I never want to have anything to do with you again."

"Why not?" I asked her.

She spoke slowly and deliberately. "Because you're just a despicable, bullying thief, and I loathe the sight of you!"

She turned and went to walk away, but I grabbed her arm and pulled her back.

"Wait a minute," I said. "You don't mean that. You can't say that just because you once happened to see something which wasn't meant to happen, and which anyway you weren't meant to see."

She looked me straight in the face and said, "I'd been blind about you. But in that railway carriage I suddenly saw you as you really are. You're rotten."

"But you didn't see it all," I said quickly. "He was buttoning up with my money. I didn't hit him for the sake of it—I did it because I had to. I don't hit anybody for the sake of it—I only do it when it's the only way to get along."

"Other people get along all right without that," she said.

"Listen, kid! That's the only way I know. That's the way I've always got along, because it's the only way I know. And it's a fair way, isn't it? I don't gang up on people, do I? There was one of me and one of him. There's always only one of me. That's fair enough, isn't it?"

"Quite fair," she said coldly, "except that you happen to be about twice as strong as most people, and you make good use of the fact."

"Oh, hell! Can I help that?" I asked her.

She didn't answer straight away. We stood there by the railings of a house by the side of the street. People kept passing, and once or twice they looked at us as if we were having a scene. But I had to talk. I had to straighten the thing out. I had to make the kid see the sense of things.

But she had dried up.

"Say something, kid," I said.

She lowered her head and looked down at the pavement. "I've got nothing to talk to you about. I never want to see you again."

It suddenly went through me that she meant it. I suddenly knew that here was something I could not snatch. Here was something that I wanted, and it was going; and I couldn't just take it, because it wasn't that kind of thing.

I hardly knew what I was saying. "Don't be like that about it, kid.

You don't understand. There's always been just one of me, and that's the way I've always wanted it. But not now. I've never cared a damn about any man or woman before. But, I'm different about you. I don't know why, but you get inside me in a way that I didn't know anything ever could."

I stopped. I waited for her to say something. And then a hell of a thing happened. Without any warning, she suddenly leaned toward me, and put her face down against my coat and started crying.

I didn't know what to do. I wished she would stop. You can't stand in a street with a girl crying on you. I took hold of her and shook her.

"Shut up doing that," I said.

"Oh, Bill," she sobbed, "why must you be like you are? Why can't you be like everyone else? Why can't you leave people alone and do a decent job? Why can't you earn a respectable living like—like—well, like the men who work in Benny's?"

Suddenly the whole place seemed to swim. I could see that high-collared slop bowing over me in the shop that afternoon. I could see all the mugs in the world lined up in front of me. I could see a few shillings being handed out at the end of the week. And here was a sniveling bitch trying to hook me into that.

I pushed her away.

"You go to hell!" I said.

Without another look at her I strode off down the street. I felt clammy. I felt as if I'd just come out from somewhere by the skin of my teeth. I strode off along the street without looking left or right, without hardly looking where I was going. My head was tight inside. The inside of it felt as if it were pressing hard against the outside. I started to tremble a bit. I clenched my hands and then I loosened them and then I clenched them again. I walked with a stiff, quick stride, getting quicker and quicker. By God! You wanted something, and then it turned out to be muck. You wanted something, and then suddenly you didn't want it anymore. But you did really. You wanted it, but you wished it weren't what it was. You wished it were different so that you could want it without wishing you didn't want it.

To hell with it all! A man had to learn to keep out of a slobbing jam like that. A man who let himself get tripped up by a bitch was just a pile. Not me. But it was different. This wasn't the usual. This wasn't the sudden spurting feeling that you get from a tart. This was different. This was inside the top half of your body somewhere. This was in your head. This was something that made you want to tear yourself in half and get it out of you.

I walked on, street after street, getting in a sweat. I could have slammed that kid's face in if I had it here in front of me now. I could have slammed anyone's face in.

I went round a corner full tilt, and a fellow in evening dress came slap into me. I pushed him back and swore at him. By God, I was in the mood all right. I looked at his face for a second, and the kid's face swam in front of my eyes. This was the kid. So I hit for the sake of hitting, did I? Okay, Don't say anything that you can't take care of, bitch. I took a quick step forward, and drove my fist into that swimming mass of eyes and nose and mouth. The man staggered back and I let him have all I'd got. He went down on the pavement with the blood streaming out of his face. "Cheap bully, cheap bully!" the words went through my head. I picked him up on to his feet again, and as he swayed there, I drew back and put the whole weight of my body into a smash that sent him sagging down like pulp.

Suddenly I heard the shrill pipe of a police whistle. I looked up, and there a couple of hundred yards away was a copper running. I took one quick glance backward and the road that way was clear. I dropped to my knees by the side of the man and felt quickly for a wallet. I found it, and pulled it out and shoved it into my pocket.

As I got to my feet the copper was getting close. I turned in the opposite direction and went down the street like a hare.

But it wasn't my lucky night. As I went across the street, a car came flashing around the corner and I couldn't get out of its way in time. I felt the sickening thud of it against me. I knew I was spinning in the air toward the curb. And then the street went round and round and round and I couldn't stop it.

As I gradually came back to consciousness, I could feel that I was moving. I could feel the swift, swaying, slightly jolting movement of a motorcar. I opened my eyes, but I was very dizzy. For a few moments everything was a confused blur. Then, as my eyes started to focus, I made out a copper. And there was a woman in white. A nurse. And there was another man; he was in white too. A doctor. I was in an ambulance with a copper and a nurse and a doctor. I was hurt. I was an ambulance case. I must be pretty badly injured.

But the nurse and the doctor weren't looking at me much. Their backs were toward me, and they were looking down away from me, the other side of the room, the other side of the ambulance. Only the copper was looking at me. He was looking at me hard. He kept fading away a bit, and then there he was clear again, still looking at me hard.

"He's coming round," I heard him say.

The doctor answered him without even glancing at me. "He'll be all right. Only knocked out and bruised a bit. We'll check him over when we get inside, but I think he'll be all right. I wish I could stop this bleeding."

I struggled to keep the place in focus, like you do when the drink is just about to pass you out, and I said, "Is that me? Is it me that's all right? Then pitch me out of this sick-van, can't you?"

"You're staying with me," the copper answered.

I tried to sit up, but my head was heavy. "You can't keep me here if I'm all right," I said.

The copper jerked his head toward the other side of the van.

"Take a look," he said.

I rolled my head over so that I could see where he meant. At first all I could see were the white backs of the nurse and the doctor, who were bending over and seemed to be doing plenty. And then suddenly the doctor moved away to reach for something, and I could see the other bunk. The top of it was red. It was just all red, and in the middle of it was the reddest thing of all, and that was a face. I looked at it hard, but it started to swim. It wasn't the blood. I can stand all the blood that's going. It wasn't the blood, I was dizzy before I looked. But as I raised my hand to hold my head steady, I saw that my hand was red just like that too. I suddenly wanted to be sick. But as I dropped my hand, the place all went swimming, and I was off again.

I sat alone in that cold room and told that fellow he wasn't so much of a mug after all. He might have kicked in, so the coppers had told me. But he wasn't going to. Now, the coppers said he wasn't going to die. He was picking up fast, like a fellow with more guts than you'd have taken him for.

I told them to send him a message from me. "Tell him from me what a good job it is he didn't kick in." But they didn't seem to see it that way much. It would have served me right, would it? I held myself tight while he said so, and tried to remember his face. You'd got to lay off while you were in the jam like this, because anything you did they would just build up against you. But if you could just tie your mind on to a face or two, you never could say but one day you might meet it on the street.

But it was bad enough. The copper said he had seen me beat the fellow up. They had found a woman who said she had seen it out of the window. The mug's wallet was in my pocket. It was bad enough.

I shrugged my shoulders, and looked around the cold stone walls.

How much would they give me? Three months? It would pass pretty quickly. But it might me more. Six months? I couldn't remember the kind of lot they were likely to hand out. You play your luck so hard, and it lasts so long, that you get to thinking it can't flop. The jab is for the others, you tell yourself. Somehow or other you'll manage to get by. The jam is for the others, for the mugs. And after a bit you put it right out of your mind and don't worry anymore. But here it is, just the same. Here it is, and this time it's you. And it's such a long time since you gave it a thought that there's nothing to do but to wait and see the way they work it out.

By the time the day of the trial came I wasn't caring a damn any more. It would pass quick enough. Anything makes a change. I was sick of kicking my heels waiting. Just tell me, that's all. If this is the way things go, then come on. Who's waiting for what?

But it all takes time. I stood in the dock in that gloomy court, while they all went through the thing over and over again. The copper saying his piece. The woman in the window saying hers. The mug mumbling his through the bandages round his face. Me saying they're all bloody liars. Round and round it goes. Not a soul in that place doesn't know that they've got it all set for me. But round and round it goes. The white-wig who's booked up for my side trying to catch the copper out, trying to make me out to be such a mug myself that in the end I have to tell him to freeze it up a bit.

At last they get to the end, and the judge pushes out his little lecture. "You have been found guilty of a despicable, brutal crime. You should consider yourself extremely lucky that you are not at this moment being tried for murder...."

His croaky voice goes on and on, and it isn't worth listening to. But the silence in the rest of the place begins to give you the creeps. I looked this way and that way, but his voice seemed to follow me around.

And suddenly I tightened. Suddenly my eyes were fixed on him and my ears were listening hard.

"… and to receive," he was saying slowly, "ten strokes with the cat-o'-nine-tails."

I stood there feeling suddenly hotter. I looked at him, and he was looking me straight in the eyes. I licked my lips. That's what he said. I looked at him hard. Yes, that's what he said. That's what he said.

Suddenly the dead silence of the place was broken by a voice, a little sobbing cry. I snatched my eyes from the judge and looked up to the gallery to find her.

There she was. God knows how she got there. God knows how the hell she knew. But there she was, with her lips trembling and her eyes all soft. I looked right through and into her. I felt the strength draining out of me, as hands took hold of my arms and led me away.

Chapter Six: MILLIONS OF EYES

Everyone keeps looking at me as if I'm something funny. The coppers and the warders all look at me as if there's something strange about me. And sometimes I catch them looking at each other, signaling something they're thinking about me. But they won't talk. They won't hardly open their mouths to me.

They point with their eyes. Yes—that's what they're doing, they're pointing with their eyes. As if I'm on show. As if I'm cooped up here as a something for people to see and examine.

"I can take it!" I tell them fiercely. That's the trouble. That's what they're thinking. They're telling themselves that I don't know what I'm in for. They're telling each other it'll crack me. That's what it is. I can see it. It shows in their faces. It shows in the way they won't open up their mouths.

"Have you ever seen it done?"

They don't answer. One by one I ask them, but they don't answer properly. They shake their heads. Their faces look like lumps of wood.

"I'm tough, d'you see?" I bellow it at them, but they won't be drawn. They're putting on the screw with this silence of theirs. It makes you wonder a bit. It makes you not quite so sure.

"Is it you that's going to give it me?" The heads shake harder than usual, but that's all. They're not giving anything away.

"Who does it? Who'll be there? Who'll see it?" Not that it matters a damn, but there's nothing to do in this place except to think around in circles.

She'll know. Already she knows I'm going to get it, because she heard. But will she know when? Will she know when it's happened? Will they tell her I took it laughing? No. There's nobody to tell her. But I will. I'll tell her quick enough when I get the chance. I'll tell her I laughed in their faces. I'll tell her it was like mice trying to bite a dog. I'll tell her it tickled and that was about all.

I'll tell her. Back there in the court it was only a threat. It was just a threat, and they'd got me fixed so that I couldn't do anything about it. She could see that. It was all right up to there. But don't let her carry in her mind any pictures of me being knocked about by anybody. No, don't let her see that. Somebody tell her that it didn't happen after all. Somebody tell her that they didn't dare. Go on, somebody. Tell her that, so that I'll be able to face her again.

Like a schoolboy, eh? Like a dog that's messed the carpet. Like a man who's lost his size. But just let her flicker one eyelid at me and I'll kill her.

It was cold earlier, but not now. As I pass my hand across my forehead it is slightly damp. It won't be long now. This morning, quite soon.

Quite soon. No putting it off. You can't choose the day. You can't wait and pick a day when you feel like it. This is their show. They do the choosing. They do everything. You're just the thing they do it with.

But it's only the damned powerless feeling, that's all. They usually scream, do they? Just mugs. They've screamed when I've hit them, but they've never really hurt me. They've picked the wrong one this time. They can knock me silly but they can't hurt me. Not the way they mean.

The footsteps clatter along the passage. Now for it. Here goes. Brace yourself. Stop those damned silly doubts from flashing across your mind. The stories about it are all the same. It isn't any picnic. So brace yourself. Face up, that's the thing.

They take me out of the cell and down the passage. They take me along, and stand me still while a man looks me up and down. He's a doctor. He gets his listening tube and tries my heart. I can feel it's beating rather quickly, rather hard. But that's just the excitement. They need a doctor, do they? They think it's that tough? My heart beats faster, but the doctor nods that I'm okay.

Now the setup is all ready. It's a gang job right enough. Five of them there. One of them is signaling directions, pointing here, there, here again. He's the boss in charge. He doesn't even speak to give his orders. His face is like stone, and for a second I feel I'd like to smash it for him. But it's only a feeling. I haven't got the chance to start things now. This is their turn. This is their show.

The place is quiet and creepy. They don't hurry. They go about the thing with cold deliberation. They can take their time. They've got me jammed, and they know they can take their time.

My eyes go round the room, and there's the fellow with it in his hands. It's got a sickly look. It's long and thin and strong, and it's got lumps on the end. It looks bad enough.

So that's the one who does it? I look at him carefully. Just let me meet him one day. He's going to hit me and get nothing back. Now—yes. But just let me meet him outside of here one day.

Come on, now. Off with my shirt. All right. Make the most of it, you slobs. Tread me down while you've got the chance. I'll play. I know this is something I can't duck. But make the most of it, in case next time it's me that's doing the work.

Feet here. Does that suit you? Please yourselves. You'd better strap them tight. Now my hands. Yes—tie them together. Tie them together good and hard and safe. You never know. You never quite know. Tie them together tight and safe.

Now we're ready. Now everything's fine. Now I'm all nicely trussed up and you can take your time.

Have a good look. It's me that's tied up here. Me. Yes, have a good look and make the most of it.

As the thing swished through the air behind me, instinct made me try to move forward with it to soften the blow. But the frame I was tied to made it impossible. I was fixed there stiff.

I heard the dull clatter of it on my back. For a fraction of a second that was all. And then a searing pain went through me. I caught my breath. My heart pounded. The wall in front of me seemed to come toward me and then fade back again.

My back was on fire. Wild claws were tearing at my flesh. It throbbed and stabbed and echoed with pain.

I clenched my teeth together. Ten of those. That was one. Nine more of these to come. By God, they knew the way to hurt. This wasn't hitting. It was just plain torture. My mouth was dry, and I breathed quickly.

Again. For a moment nothing, and then I was wrenching at the cords round my wrists in a frenzy of pain. It shot through me and into me, tearing madly at my whole body. The blood came roaring rough my head and I was half blinded. The wall front of me was swaying.

No more! No more! Oh, God! keep quiet! Never mind your back, keep your teeth together. Never mind that god-awful pain, keep your teeth together. Let them apart for a second and you'll shout. Anybody would. Oh, God! yes, anybody would. Keep them together. Harder. Tighter. Bite, you fool. Bite!

Again. The ravaging smart tears up and down me. For an awful moment I think I've come in half. It's through my flesh. It's in my spine. I'm going to snap and my head is going to burst.

Again. I tear at my wrists like a madman. Just give me one smash at this swine with the whip and I'll stop him forever. I'll kill him. I'll kill them all. I'll tear them all to pieces.

They won't come. My hands won't come. I tear and strain at them until my wrists start to bleed, but they won't come. The blood comes trickling down my arms, but the pain is all one with the rest of me. It doesn't end anywhere. I'm just all shapeless pain all over the place.

Again. Oh, God! no more! Doesn't it stop anywhere? Do I have to stay tied up here while they kill me? Let me get away. Just let me get away. Let me give it to them like this. Anybody. Let me get hold of somebody, quick. Now. Let me get hold of somebody and tear the bloody guts right out of them. Just like they're tearing the bloody guts right out of me.

Again. No. Shut up. Bite, can't you? Teeth together. Harder. Tighter. It can't go on. It can't get any worse. It's just all throbbing, tearing pain. That's all it is. That's all everything is. Come on. Harder. In and out. Round and round. That's all it is. That's all it is.

Was that it again? It's all the same now. It's all one great big stabbing pain. You can't get away. They never stop. It's like this always now. On and on. Just waves of burning sweat and blood. But less and less. Like the wall in front of you, less and less and less.

They've stopped. Have they? You can't be quite sure, because it feels just the same now, whether they go on or whether they stop. But they must have stopped; they're letting my wrists and feet loose. And now they're hanging on to me, to prevent me from slopping on the floor.

The winter came, and dragged right through, and went again. You knew it was winter because it was colder, and the skies when you saw them were nearly always covered over, and it got dark early. Those were the ways you had of knowing now. Those were the things that prison couldn't hide from you. It could take everything else. It could take away your touch with life. It could stop you from seeing and hearing and feeling the pulse of the world. It could kill the inside of you. It could make you stay still when everything inside you was pushing you to get moving. It could make you move when everything inside you was tugging you to stay still.

I was one of two things. Either I was inside that three-walled room with the bars at the end, or I was outside it. That was the only difference. Life hadn't any details now. There weren't any ifs and buts. You didn't make your mind up anymore. That happened automatically. You didn't decide things now. You didn't hate things or like things now. You didn't funk things or face up to things. You didn't make your mind up. It was automatic. It was when a whistle blew. You didn't hate anymore, because there wasn't any point, because you couldn't run away. You didn't want things anymore; it was just a waste of thinking, because you couldn't reach out and grab. You didn't think, you didn't make your mind up anymore. A whistle did that for you. You were walking and you heard a whistle, and you stopped. That was fine. That was the idea. You stopped when you heard the whistle, and everything was fine.

Life was made up of two things: going through the gate out of the room, and going through the gate into the room. And either was the worst every time it happened.

It would be time to go out. To exercise, to work, to eat? That didn't matter.

"Come on!"

It was time to go out. Never mind what for. It was time to go out. Time to go out and feel the eyes: the hundreds of eyes, the millions of eyes.

"Come on!"

I got up and stepped through the gate into the passage. I stepped warily, taut, like a cat. Perhaps if I went very stealthily I could escape them. Perhaps they wouldn't hear me coming. Perhaps they'd forget. Perhaps they just wouldn't remember for once.

But it wasn't any good. Twenty yards down the passage and they were on me. I could feel their eyes going through me, looking at me bare, stripped, and helpless.

There he is!

It's me they mean. And they're not even saying it. That wouldn't be so bad, but they're not even saying it. It's their eyes that at saying it. Their millions of eyes. Over and over again.

They tied him up and gave it to him.... Like a dog, like an animal.... Yes, it was him.... Ha! Ha! Ha! You should have seen it.... Never saw anyone get such a good thrashing.... The man with the whip had a lovely time.... With all the strength he'd got, and nobody hitting back.... No fear of anybody hitting back, because it was him, all cowed and collapsing.... Yes, that's him there.... They thrashed him to pulp and he couldn't even hit back.... Ha! Ha! Ha! His back was all soft and juicy.... Yes, there he is!

All the time. I can feel their eyes saying it, and they never stop. They aren't even looking at me, but their eyes are saying it. I can feel them saying it all the time. I can feel them going through me and tearing me open and laughing.

But it's over for now. It's time to go back. Now I can get away from them for a bit, thank God! It's time to go back.

"Go on!"

I hesitate at the gate into the room. For a desperate moment I wonder if I can cut and run. But it isn't any good.

"Go on!"

I tighten myself, and step slowly into the cell. The gate shuts behind me, and the place crowds on to me in a sudden crashing roar. My head starts to press and strain inside, and I rush at the walls and try to push them away to give myself room. It's on top of me. It's pressing me in. It's tying me up. I can feel my wrists, bound tight and helpless together. I can feel them straining and tearing to get free. I can feel the blood trickling down my arms, the veins standing out, the sweat and the blood and the agony in my back.

"Bite, you fool!"

The place is crowding in on me, pressing me in and treading me down. Through the rush and the roar of the din in my head I hear people shouting: "Turn it off!"

"Fer Gawd's sake, gag 'im, somebody!"

The voices of other prisoners come floating vaguely down the passage. And then the steps of the warders and the curt voices coming through the bars.

In a frenzy I fight to free myself. I stretch my arms wide apart, left and right, as far as I can get them. But they still feel tied together. I stretch them apart until my shoulders ache, but they still feel tied together.

The din gathers, getting louder and louder, until at last something gives way somewhere, and I lie down and go sobbingly to sleep.

But somehow or other the winter came and dragged right through and went again, and some of the pains became aches, and some of the sounds were half in the distance now, and there is somebody to see me. Yes, one day there is somebody to see me.

"Your first visitor," the warder said, "and it' a lady."

So she'd come to see me, had she? She'd come to say, "I told you so." She'd come to look at me, and put her eyes all over me, and look for the marks and make sure I was sorry.

"I don't want to see her," I said.

The warder looked surprised. "Come on, Saunders, snap out of it!" he said. He wasn't so bad.

"I don't want to see her," I told him.

He shrugged his shoulders and turned around and started to walk away. I called him back.

"Just a minute," I said, "where do I see her?"

"This way," he said.

I followed him, through the gates and along the passages and round the corners, and suddenly there she was. She was dressed in different clothes that I hadn't seen before, and her hair was done in a different way, and the look on her face was different, but she was just the same. When you looked hard, she was just the same.

"Hullo, Bill!" she said.

I didn't answer. I fixed my eyes on hers and looked right into them. I was watching for a look. I was watching for her eyes to go searching over me. I was watching for "I told you so," but it didn't come. It wasn't there. She was just the same. She was looking at me as if it were only yesterday, and she was friendly again.

She looked at me softly and simply, as if I wasn't something strange, as if everything were natural.

"Hullo, Bill!" she said again.

"Hullo!" I said. "Why did you come?"

She smiled. She was just the same.

"Why did I come before, you mean?"

"No," I said. "Why did you come now?"

"I came to say hullo," she said. "I've been meaning to come all the time, but somehow I haven't."

"Why did you want to see me anymore?" I asked.

"Let's leave the difficult questions out," she said, and smiled again. "You're looking fine, Bill."

"So are you," I said.

We both stopped talking. It was difficult to think of much to say. After a bit she said, "I'm still at Benny's."

"Who waits outside for you now?" I asked.

She wiped off the smile. "Don't talk like that, Bill," she said.

"Well, it's certainly not me," I said.

She smiled again, and as casually as if it were all the most natural thing in the world, she asked, "How long will you be now?"

I shrugged my shoulders, and made a face, because something in the way the skin had gone made my back tickle every time I shrugged my shoulders.

"Not so very long," I said.

"Have you got any plans, Bill?"

"How do you mean?"

"Have you got any plans for—then?"

I shook my head. "Why should I have?" I asked her.

"Oh, I don't know," she said; "I just wondered." And then she looked me straight in the face and said, "I've been doing a lot of thinking since that day in court. Will you do me two favors?"

"I can't do many here," I said.

"You can do these," she said.

"Why, what are they?"

She hesitated, and then she said, "The first is, will you forget what I said that night in the street when I cried? And the second is, will you let me try to make some plans?"

I looked at her, puzzled. "I don't get you," I said.

She smiled. The warder came up behind her and touched her arm, and motioned with his head that she had to go.

"See you again soon, Bill," she said.

"Goodbye," I said; and then, just as she was going, I said, "Thanks for coming, kid. And thanks for not coming before."

I turned away and went back with the warder. And all along the passages and still all that day and all that night, the only eyes that looked at me were hers.

She came many times after that, and life began to take a bit of shape again. There were certain fixed dates when she was allowed to come, and that gave the thing a bit of shape. Time wasn't just endless anymore. Now, I could measure it out by how long it was since she came last, and how long it would be before she'd be coming again. I used to work it out and count it up and tick off the difference each day, and it gave life a shape. Sometimes we talked a lot, and sometimes we hardly talked at all. But she always came. Gradually it became clear that she was trying to fix up something for me to do when I got out. When I first tumbled to this, I shied off the idea pretty fast. She was sticking her nose too far into my business, and I told her so. But she looked so disappointed that I had to ease up about it. If it kept her happy, thinking about things like that, then she might as well. And anyway, I couldn't be too strong about it, in case she stopped coming. I tried laughing it off. "Perhaps I could get a job near here," I suggested, "so that I'll be handy in case they want me back again." But she didn't like that. She was very serious about it.

Then one day she arrived absolutely bubbling with excitement. "I've got everything arranged," she said eagerly, as I arrived with the warder.

"Let's have it," I said, getting ready to laugh. But when she told me what it was, it was even too much to laugh at.

"I have an old aunt," she said, "who lives in the country with a lot of chickens and things, and sells eggs and butter direct to people. And she has promised to give you a job. She doesn't know anything about you, except that you are a friend of mine. I have told her that you are arriving from abroad. It's not that I'm ashamed," she added quickly. "Of course it isn't anything like that, Bill. But she is rather an old-fashioned old dear, and I thought it might be best if I told her that."

She stopped, and looked at me with eager eyes and her lips apart. I looked back at her dully. She meant it, and she was excited about it, and she had come to see me, and she had given life a shape again, and she was quite a part of everything by now. But—me with eggs! I searched her, but she was serious right enough. I looked at her hard, but she wasn't trying to poke me.

I felt it was up to me to say something, but I couldn't think what. "How do you mean?" I asked.

"Well, Bill," she said, "you see, she has got an old car for bringing the produce into town and delivering it round the houses. She has to have someone to drive it, because she has so much to do at the farm that she hasn't time to drive it herself. And the man she has now wants to leave because he is going to set up on his own, and I thought perhaps you could do it. You can drive, can't you?"

I nodded. "Yes, I can drive all right," I admitted, "but I've never driven eggs before."

She looked so pleased about the whole thing that I didn't want to spoil it for her by bumping her.

"You see, Bill," she went on quickly, "you would be out and about, you would be moving all the time, and you wouldn't feel cooped up at all, and it might be rather fun, and it would be something to do for a bit anyway, wouldn't it?"

"Me and eggs," I murmured to myself.

"Oh, but, Bill, it just happens to be eggs, but that doesn't make any difference. It might be anything. And anyway, I have told her about you, and she'll be expecting you. You're not going to let me down about it, are you, Bill?"

I hesitated. "When?" I asked her.

"It's only two months now, isn't it?"

"That's all," I said.

"You haven't got anything else in mind, have you?" she asked.

I shook my head. Her eyes were shining. You couldn't just bluntly say no to the kid when she was so happy about something.

"I'll think about it," I said.

After she had gone, it kept hanging round in my mind. Me and eggs. It was funny. It was so damned funny that I kept laughing. But it went on hanging round in my mind. Me and eggs might be better than me and nothing.

Chapter Seven: THE NEW LINE

"Remember, you've come from Canada," she said. "I don't think it will be difficult, because Auntie's never been out of England, so she won't know many awkward questions to ask." She laughed, "You'd better learn up some names of places as soon as you can, in case you do bump into someone round here who has been there, and starts to talk about it."

"If I do, I can soon shut them up," I said.

The bus stopped in the village, and we got down. It was Sunday morning and the place looked sleepy and rather one-eyed.

"It's about a mile to walk now," she said.

We set off along the lane, and had soon left the village behind. The fields stretched away on both sides of the lane. The sun was bright and warm; it gave you a sense of freedom to be out here without any people watching you or crowding round you. We strode faster and faster and I began to feel fine.

"Slow up a bit," said the kid. "I'm getting puffed, you're going at such a speed."

"Sorry, " I said, "but it was your idea, all this."

She laughed. "It's a nice idea, and you're going to like it," she said. "Just you get that into your head, mister." She had a way of saying things that you wouldn't let anyone else say to you.

We went on walking for about twenty minutes, and then we came round a corner and saw a little brick house with one or two sheds clustered loosely round it.

"That's it," she said, and waved her hand. "And that's Auntie."

Her aunt was a middle-aged woman with gray hair and a face that looked as if she could be a lot of nuisance if she didn't get her own way. She came out to the gate to meet us, walking in an easy, masculine way. She was strong, and good for her age, as far as you could see.

She smiled and held out both hands to the kid.

"So glad to see you, Jane, dear," she said. Then she turned to me. "So this is the young man you were telling me about?" She gave me a friendly smile.

"Yes, this is Mr. Saunders," said the kid. "Bill, this is Mrs. Wharton, my aunt."

"Second aunt," corrected Mrs. Wharton, and held out her hand to me. "How do you do?" she asked.

"I'm fine," I said.

She looked me up and down in a way that asked for her to be told to mind her own business, but I caught the kid's eye and I smiled. This was a deal. This was a thing between me and the kid, and nobody else's business. This was something I had promised her. This was the only way of keeping to know the kid, and it was worth having a go at.

"So Jane has told you all about my little business, Mr. Saunders?" she said.

"She's told me about the eggs," I answered.

She smiled. "Well, you've just arrived at feeding time. I must see to it before we have our tea, so you may as well come and look round with me."

She led the way over to one of the outbuildings, and went inside and picked up a tin of grain. There were chickens all over the place, and they knew it was feeding-time because they started kicking up a racket as soon as she came out of the shed.

We watched her scattering handfuls of the stuff in all directions until she had used it all up. Then she took the empty tin back into the hut and shut the door.

"Now they are happy," she said. "Let's just have a look and see what they have done to earn their keep."

She went over to a little hut with a sloping roof and looked inside it. Then she bent down and scuffled about, and handed us up some eggs. I took one in my hands. It was still warm.

"Half a minute," said the kid's aunt. "I'll get the basket."

She went off toward the house and came back in a minute with a big open basket. Then she led the way round a lot of little huts with the sloping roofs, and by the time she had finished, the basket I was carrying was full.

I stood there, wondering what to do with it. "I expect you are ready for some tea now," said Mrs. Wharton. She moved off toward the house.

I looked, at her, and looked at the kid, and looked at the basket of eggs in my hands. Well, why not? I could carry a basket of eggs as well as either of them could. I followed them into the house.

It was pleasant and cozy inside. The furniture was old, and there were a lot of pictures and photos on the walls, and it had the kind of feeling a place only gets after someone lives in it for a long time.

The parlor table was set with cups and saucers and plates, and in the middle of the table was a big plate piled high with bread and butter. Mrs. Wharton went out of the room to fetch the tea, leaving us alone there. I looked at the kid, and then across at the eggs, and then back at her. She smiled.

"How am I doing?" I asked her.

"You're doing very well," she said. "But surely it hasn't been very difficult so far?"

"Hasn't it?" I asked. "I might have dropped the lot, mightn't I?"

Mrs. Wharton came back into the room, carrying a big brown teapot. She put it on the table, and sat down on one of the chairs. "Come on, you two," she said. "I expect you have developed country appetites already."

We all sat down at the table and got going on the bread and butter. Out of the cupboard she produced some homemade jam. Then she looked across at me with an inquiring look in her eyes, and said, "Well, Mr. Saunders, so you have just come back from Canada?"

I looked straight back at her. "That's right," I said.

"Have you been there long?"

"Quite a time," I said.

"What were you doing out there?"

"Oh, different things," I said. I began to think perhaps the kid and I ought to have rehearsed this part a bit more, but the kid came cutting in to the rescue.

"You see, Aunt," she said quickly, "Bill's been getting a kind of general experience out there, moving about and turning his hand to anything and everything. Nothing very fixed, but just kind of feeling his way. Haven't you, Bill?"

I nodded eagerly. "Yes, that's right," I said.

"That just about describes it perfectly. Nice place you've got here, Mrs. Wharton," I added, to get the subject changed as quickly as possible.

Her face warmed. "You like it?" she said. "It wasn't much when I came to it, but I have been doing things to it all the time, and it is gradually beginning to be quite a good little chicken farm. You see, I first started off with only a handful of chickens, and I used to sell the eggs to one or two friends near where I used to live. They liked them, because they were getting them ten times as fresh as they could get them in the shops. After a time they began to tell their friends, and I found myself being asked for more and more. So I got more chickens, and then more customers came; so I got still more chickens, and now it is quite a little business. It is much more than I can do alone now, of course. I have an old car in the garage here, and a man from the village has been doing all the delivering for me, driving the eggs into town and calling at the houses with them."

She paused. The kid had been through all this to me until I was sick of hearing it, but she would not have liked it if I'd butted in and stopped her aunt from talking.

Mrs. Wharton went on. "The man is going to leave me now. He has decided to set up on his own. But I expect Jane has told you all about this, hasn't she?"

I nodded. "She has," I said.

"Well—" Mrs. Wharton hesitated, and looked at me inquiringly. Again the kid jumped in.

"Bill would love it, Aunt," she said.

"Would you, Mr. Saunders?"

"I'll do it," I said.

"Will you? I'm so glad," she said, "because it is so necessary for me to have a man I can trust, and you being a friend of Jane's makes it so nice."

I quizzed her, but her smile seemed natural enough. I smiled back. Not many people had trusted me when they had any choice about it. I suddenly liked the old girl. She was straight to the point and no slopping about.

"When do I start?" I asked her.

"As soon as you like," she said. "There is a room upstairs for you here if you want it. It would be better for you to go round for a week with Jeff—that's the man who drives the car at present—to learn the way round and get to know where all the customers live."

"Where is this Jeff man going to set up business?" asked the kid.

"He tells me there is a place about ten miles from here that he can get," said Mrs. Wharton.

"Has he got any customers?" the kid asked.

Mrs. Wharton shrugged her shoulders, and then suddenly looked at the kid with a little puzzled frown. "I don't suppose he has yet," she said. "Why?"

"Oh, I don't know," said the kid. "I suppose I ought not to think this, but it does occur to me that if he has been doing all the delivering, it might be very easy for him to start dealing with some of yours."

"Oh, I don't think he would do that," Mrs. Wharton said. "He has always been quite straight, with me."

"No, I am sure he wouldn't," said the kid. "All the same, it would be easy, wouldn't it? I mean, all that half of your customers know is that this man Jeff, or whatever his name is, drives up regularly with their eggs. After he has left you, he could still drive up regularly with their eggs, and they wouldn't notice any difference."

Mrs. Wharton looked at the kid with a reproving frown. "You

have a very suspicious mind, my dear," she said. "I don't think there is any need to worry, because Mr. Saunders will be going round with him first, and in that way he will get to know where they all live, and when they see Mr. Saunders there too, they will realize that I am having a changeover."

"Don't you worry, Mrs. Wharton," I put in. "If there is any of that, I'll soon take care of the fellow for you."

I saw the kid shoot me a look. Mrs. Wharton only smiled and said, "I am sure everything will be all right."

On the way back to town a thought struck me. "Kid," I said, "I've just seen something new on this. If I'm stuck out there with old Eggs, I won't see much of you."

She smiled, that soft smile of hers that did funny things to you. "There are the weekends," she said

"Yes," I answered, "but there are the weeks, too."

"Well, never mind," she said. "After a while, when you have shaken down into the job, perhaps you will be able to make some arrangement whereby you can have a room in town and go out to the farm every day. After all, the journey doesn't take very long."

"Do you know," I said, "I'm beginning to think this whole business is a bit of a washout after all. Being cut off in the country is not exactly my line."

"Bill, it's your *new* line," she said firmly. "And remember you have promised me that you'll give it a proper try."

She was looking very serious, but it wasn't a stiff look. She was looking the way that only she could. It had been just like that when I had promised her.

"Don't worry, kid," I said.

It was arranged that the man Jeff should leave a week after I started, and I spent the whole of the first week trundling round with him, packing up the layout of all the customers. Mrs. Wharton had given me a list of the names and addresses of all of them, and whether they were due for a delivery or not, we went round the whole lot so that I would have an easier job finding them next time on my own. There were nearly a hundred and fifty of them, and they were spread over a wide area, and as the car was rather an old crock and would not go very fast, it took a long time getting round.

I didn't like the look of Jeff much. He struck me as being a sulky-looking mug, and as we drove along he would keep starting to ask all sorts of questions about what I had been doing, which would start to get awkward at times, and often I had to hold myself in pretty tight to stop myself from shutting his mouth up for him. In the end I was getting so annoyed that I had to invent a way of cooling myself. Just as I felt my fist buckling up tight, I would shut my eyes for a moment and look at the kid. Just for a moment I would look at the kid, with that tilt on her lips and that softness in her eyes. After a bit of practice, this started to work pretty well. I could hear her say. "You promised me," and then I would cool down quickly.

But on the last day of Jeff's week, something happened. We had been taking it in turns getting out of the car and going up to the doors of the houses. Gradually, although I didn't take much notice of it at the time, Jeff had been sending me up to the doors of the houses where they wanted eggs, and for himself he had been picking out the houses where they didn't seem to want any yet. I asked him why he troubled to go to the door if he knew they wouldn't be wanting any. "Isn't the idea just to show me where they hang out?" I asked him.

"Yes," he said, "but there's no harm in just making sure."

I started to watch him more carefully, and as he was talking to the woman at one of the doors, I saw him hand her a piece of paper. If she had handed him a piece of paper it might have been an order, but it was he who handed the piece of paper to her.

When he came back to the car, I asked him what it was.

"Nothing," he said, and went to let in the clutch.

"Wait a minute," I said, and leaned forward and turned the engine off.

"What are you worrying about?" he asked.

"What was it you handed to that woman?"

He shifted his face about.

"Nothing," he said quickly. "I don't know what you are talking about. Let's get going, we're wasting time."

I opened the door of the car, and went to step out into the road. Then I suddenly turned back and took the ignition key out of the car so he couldn't start it again.

"You wait here," I told him.

I went up to the house he had just come from, and knocked on the door. A woman opened it.

"Excuse me," I said, "but I'm working for Mrs. Wharton, who sells you eggs."

She smiled. "Oh, that's all right," she said; "the other man has just been, the usual man, and he told me about the change of address."

"He told you about what?" I asked.

"He explained that Mrs. Wharton was moving, and gave me the new address to write to when I wanted some more eggs."

I felt myself tighten all over, and the weals on my back started to tickle.

"That's all I wanted to know," I said, and I turned quickly and went out into the road again.

Jeff was sitting in the car looking at me as I came out. I walked over and got into the car beside him and shut the door. Then I put the ignition key in, and switched the engine on.

"Get going," I told him.

"What's the matter, Bill?" he asked nervously.

"Shut up and drive on," I told him. "Straight back."

"Back where?"

"Back to the farm," I said.

"But we haven't finished going round yet."

"Back to the farm," I said.

"But, Bill—it was only a sort of a joke," he started.

"Shut up," I said. "Drive on and keep your mouth shut."

My hands were bunching up and I was tight all over. This was the fellow that old Eggs had trusted. What did the kid expect me to do about this? Did this come into the bargain? There was only one way to deal with this, and that was to smash him up for good so that he couldn't mess around anymore.

"Listen, Bill," he started again.

"Shut up," I whispered.

I closed my eyes and looked, and there she was. All right. I promised. But this is your way of doing things, not mine. If he's got to be allowed to get away with this kind of thing, it's your game, not mine.

We drove on in silence. Out through the edges of the town and into the country. By the side of the road I saw a big pond.

"Stop here," I told him suddenly.

He went to drive on. "What's the idea?" he asked.

I leaned forward and took the ignition key out again. The car shuddered to a standstill.

"Get out," I said.

"Don't think you can order me about," he said.

I didn't wait to argue. I took hold of his wrist and twisted it so that he yelped. Then I opened the door and dragged him out into the road.

"Leave go of my arm!" he said.

"Listen, you," I said. "For two pins I'd smash you to bits, but you're in luck today. You're in luck because you're dealing with somebody who isn't quite having his own way about it, see? But this will cool you off a bit!"

I untwisted his wrist, but before he could snatch it away I bent my knees and ducked a bit, pulling his arm quickly forward and shoving my shoulder under his armpit. Then, holding his arm down tight in front of me, I straightened my knees with a jerk and let go of his wrist at the same moment. He went sailing through the air, with his arms and legs flying, and landed smack in the middle of the pond.

He got up with the mud dripping from all over him, cursing his head off.

"And the next time it's not going to be so soft!" I shouted. Then, before he could wade out and make me lose my temper, I got into the car again and drove back to the farm.

When I told Eggs, she was worried. She was a nice old stick, and the kid was very fond of her, and when I saw how worried she was I began to wish I had been a bit tougher with the swine. But she didn't seem to be looking at it that way. She was worried in case he had done it to a lot of her customers.

"But I don't think you ought to have been quite so rough with him, Bill," she said.

"What?" I asked her.

"Well, throwing a man into a pond is a dreadful thing!" she said.

I looked at her and laughed. "Yes," I said, "it's a dreadful thing. I had to shut my eyes for a minute before I could decide to do it!"

On the Sunday I saw the kid again. We had arranged to meet halfway, at a place on the edge of the town where the houses straggled and it tried to be country. I got off the bus where we had agreed to meet, and walked up and down killing time. I was early on purpose, because I didn't want to keep her waiting. After one or two buses, the one with her in it came along. She waved to me out of the window as she got up from the seat, and stepped down on the ground, smiling at me eagerly.

"Hullo, Bill!" she said. "Isn't it a marvelous day?"

"Hullo!" I said.

She was dressed in a neat costume that I hadn't seen before, and she wore a little hat that sat on the back of her head and showed all her face, and made you want to look at her all the time.

"What's the program?" she asked.

"Anything you like," I said.

"Walking's cheap," she said, with a gay little laugh, "and I could do with some fresh air."

"Come on, then," I said.

We set off, taking the direction I had come from, and turned off down one of the side roads. Very soon we had left the straggles of the town behind. It was a lovely day, bright and shining, and for nearly half an hour we walked without hardly speaking at all. At last we came to where there was a little stream by the side of the road, with a rickety wooden bridge over it. The kid stopped.

"It's me for a rest," she said, and putting her hands on the side of the bridge, she hoisted herself up and sat with her legs dangling.

I looked at the woodwork. "Will it hold us both, do you think?" I asked her.

"Let's risk it," she said. "I can swim."

I jumped up beside her, and we sat there over the water with the sun on our faces.

"Well," she said, "how's the job going?"

"It's going all right," I said.

"Is that all you have to tell me about it?" she asked.

So then I told her about Jeff, and how I had found out what his game was, and how I had chucked him into the pond. She listened all through without interrupting, and when I had finished telling her about it, she still sat quiet for a moment or two. Then she turned and looked at me.

"That's true, isn't it, Bill?" she said, as if she wanted to believe it all, but wasn't quite sure.

"Why shouldn't it be?" I asked.

"I mean, it's true about throwing him into the pond?" she asked. I nodded.

"You didn't hit him, did you, Bill?"

"No," I said. "I did what I told you, that's all."

She looked at me softly, and then as I sat there with my legs dangling and my hands on the top of the wooden parapet, I felt her hand rest on mine, and she said in a quiet, steady little voice, "I'm glad you didn't, Bill." And then: "I think he deserved the pond."

"He deserved more than that," I said. "He deserved smashing up, good and hard."

But she shook her head, and her hand pressed ever so slightly down on mine.

"I think he deserved the pond," she said again. "Somehow or other I thought we were going to have some trouble of that kind. I don't know why. I've never even seen this Jeff, but for some reason or other it just happened to cross my mind directly Aunt spoke about it."

"Eggs is pretty worried about it," I said.

"Eggs?"

"Your aunt," I said.

"Surely you don't call her Eggs, Bill!" she exclaimed.

"Not to her face," I laughed, "but she'll always be Eggs to me. Don't worry; she and I are getting on fine."

"I suppose she's worried in case Jeff has been trying to steal a lot of her customers?"

"That's the trouble," I said. "You see, a lot of these people, especially the ones who live rather out of the way, drop her a post card saying when they would like some eggs, and then sometimes they drop her a post card telling her about some friend of theirs who would also like to start buying eggs from her. She's afraid that a lot of these post cards may be going to the wrong address now."

"And you can't tell if he told that to any others or not?"

I shook my head.

"I jumped on him as soon as I spotted it," I said. "But he may have been doing it all the time without my noticing it, because I wasn't looking for it."

"Poor old aunt!" said the kid. "It seems such a shame for anyone to trick such a nice, trusting person."

"Just let me catch him on the job again," I said, "and I'll give him something to remember."

The kid looked serious. "Do be careful, Bill," she said. "For one thing, however much he deserved anything, the police are not going to be any too eager to believe your side of the story. And besides—" She paused, and looked at me steadily. And then she seemed to change her mind, because she didn't go on to finish her sentence at all.

I searched her face and wondered. Not for anyone else had I ever stopped pleasing myself. Not for anyone else had I ever waited to think twice. Yet now, with the kid, it almost seemed like pleasing myself to be pleasing her. I wondered what it was. I searched her, but it was hard to decide what it was. Just the uptilted nose and the soft eyes and the mouth with that curious twist at the corner which made you think she was going to smile any minute.

I slid off the parapet, down onto the bridge. "What about going to find somewhere to eat?" I asked.

"Rather! I'm starving," she said.

I put up my hands and held her by the elbows and lifted her gently down. She smiled at me as I held her.

"You're strong, aren't you, Bill?" She said it as if it were good for me to be strong—as if she liked it. I remembered that time in the street, the night before I got in the jam. Then, she had said how strong I was in a way that sounded as if she hated me for it. But it was different now. A lot of things were different now. I looked at her and wondered, but I couldn't see what it was.

We set off again down the road, walking slowly now. Soon we came to a village, with just a double line of cottages and a little general shop and a pub. The shop was closed.

"We shan't get anything to eat in this place," I said.

"Couldn't we get something in the pub?" she suggested.

"We could try," I answered.

We walked through the gate and across the little strip of garden that separated it from the road. The door opened straight into a stone-floored parlor with a little bar at one end of it. There was only a couple of villagers sitting there, and a man behind the bar.

"Can we get anything to eat?" I asked him.

"We can give you some bread and cheese," he answered. "Good morning, miss."

"Good morning," said the kid. "That sounds lovely, doesn't it, Bill?"

"Will that do for you?" I asked her.

"Rather!" she said. "It's just what I fancy."

"Bread and cheese for two?" said the man, as if to get a final checkup before actually producing anything. "Like any onions with it?"

"I'd love some, if you'll have them too," she said.

"Onions," I said to him.

We sat down at a little table in the middle of the parlor, and waited for the bread and cheese and onions to arrive.

"Like a drink?" I asked her.

"May I have a glass of beer?"

"Two bitters," I told the man.

The walk had given us both an appetite. The bread was new, with a crackly crust, and we both tucked into it fast.

"Let's have some more," I said, when we had both cleared our plates.

"I shall probably burst, but I'll risk it," she laughed.

The man brought two more hunks of bread and two more pieces of cheese, and by the time we were nearing the end of it, she was slowing down a lot as if she was feeling it.

"If I ate like that every day, I'd soon be like a balloon," she said.

"You'll soon walk that off," I said. "Remember we've got quite a longish way to go back."

For a while we sat in the quiet bar, and with the food and the warm day we were both a bit drowsy. We were about ready for a snooze, but it came to two o'clock and we had to get out because the pub was closing.

We set off walking slowly back, and by the time we got to where the buses were, it was nearly four o'clock.

"Like some tea?" I asked her.

"If you can wait until we get back to my room I'll make you some there," she said.

"I can wait all right," I said. "We'll get the next bus."

We went on the bus into town. It landed us quite near to where she lived, and only left us a few minutes' walk to her room.

She unlocked the door and let me in, and I looked around it with a smile. It was a long time.

She went straight over and started filling the kettle.

"It's a long time since I was here," I said.

"Yes," she said.

"I didn't hardly think I'd be coming again."

"No."

I stood there with a sudden strange awkwardness on me, while she lit the gas ring and put the kettle on. The room looked just the same, with the bed she had laid on all night in her clothes, and the corner by the door where I had dozed. As my mind went back to it all, I felt uncomfortable, and wished I had not come.

She was quiet, as if she felt something too. When she had finished laying out the cups and plates and putting the tea in the pot, she said, "No. That time, I didn't think you would be coming again either."

"I had to be pretty rough with you that night," I tried to explain; but she cut me short.

"I didn't mean that," she said.

But there was something about the place that butted in between us. We both seemed to feel ill at ease about it, and I was glad when the kettle boiled and she made the tea, so that we could sit down and have something definite to look at. We started and finished our tea in silence, but I could sense that she was still thinking about that night. It seemed to be growing up like a cloud. As we sat there, we both knew that we were both thinking about it. Without a word, without a glance, we both knew. It hung over us, heavy and threatening. So much had happened since, she knew so much about me now. That one evening back in the past couldn't matter anymore. But that wasn't true. At the back of my mind I knew that wasn't true. A man had died that night because I had hit him. She didn't know that. I had told her, straight out clearly, that it hadn't been me. She didn't know. And yet, with both of us here together in that room again, our minds were going backward in the silence, and the cloud was there. That was the one thing she must never know. I had seen her face go hard and bitter and hating, and I had seen it soft again. But that was the one thing she would never be able to forgive.

When she spoke, to me it seemed to crash the silence like a bomb. "May I have a cigarette, please, Bill?"

I fumbled for the packet, and opened it for her. As I held the match, her eyes met mine. They were distant, with the spell of that room between us.

It had to be broken. "Funny," I said, "what a lot can come out of a casual thing like me ducking here that night."

She leaned forward to reach the flame, and puffed her cigarette alight.

"Thanks," she said. And as if she had not heard me at all, she got to her feet, and said, "Mind if I rinse these few things straight away? I hate leaving messy cups and plates about."

After she had busied about, washing the cups and plates at the washbasin that did service as a sink as well, she sat down again and started to talk about how nice the walk in the country had been. But the talking was stiff. The room still seemed to be butting in between us, and I felt I wanted to go. Not back to the farm yet— that wasn't what I wanted, but just to get out of this room. There wasn't any hurry to get back to the farm. Sitting out there in the evening, with the deadly quiet all around was a thing to give you the shivers, and I knew I wouldn't be able to stick it for long. Perhaps I could go on sticking the work if it pleased the kid, but I wouldn't be able to go on living and sleeping out there. Very soon I would have to get myself somewhere in town to sleep. And it might turn out that in a different room this peculiar something wouldn't come pushing itself in between us.

"I'm going to get myself a room in town somewhere," I said.

She looked surprised. "But you've hardly given yourself time to look around there," she said.

"I've had more time than I need," I said. "It's all right in the daytime. Doing the work is all right. But it gets me down in the evenings and the nights; it's too quiet and cut off. I'm going to get myself a bed in town straight away."

"But isn't it going to make rather a hole in your money?" she asked.

"But you yourself suggested it in the first place," I reminded her. "Besides, I shan't spend much on it. I can get a cheap room somewhere, just enough sleep in. I've mentioned it to Eggs already, and I can drive the car in with a load full in the evenings, and then I'm all ready to start delivering the next morning."

"But why not wait a little while?" she suggested. "There's no hurry, is there?"

"What's the point of waiting?" I asked. "If I'm going to do it, I might as well do it now."

I knew the reason, and she must have been able to guess the reason too. I could see her in the evenings then. Stuck out at the farm, I could only see her now and again. But if I had a room in town, I could see her in the evenings. And I wanted somewhere to see her apart from this room of hers. It was making us both feel strange, and it was taking the fun out of the afternoon.

I got up as if to go. She didn't want to stop me.

"I think I'll be off," I said.

"All right, Bill."

She was standing there close to me, with her face looking up into mine. Something went stabbing through me, and wanted to take her and grab hold of her and melt her into me. But she wasn't like that. You couldn't treat her as if she were a tart. I didn't quite know what to do with her. I put out my hands and held her very gently by the shoulders.

"So long!" I said.

"So long, Bill!" she answered softly, still looking at me. Suddenly I put my head down and kissed her on the mouth. I kissed her lightly, just touching her, as if she were something fragile that I didn't want to spoil. And then, without knowing why, without really understanding what was inside me, I took my hands off her shoulders, turned round and grabbed my hat, and walked out of the room and shut the door behind me. Then I went through the front door into the street, and walked quickly away.

Chapter Eight: NOT LIKE ANYONE ELSE

I had made up my mind to lose no time in getting myself some kind of a spot in town, and on the Tuesday, when I was in there with the car, I drove round to a cheap district about a mile from where the kid lived. At one of those newsagents' shops, with the outside plastered with envelopes advertising rooms, I soon found what I wanted. There was a room "for a gentleman only" for twelve shillings a week. I went along to see it, and took it on the spot. It was a scruffy place, in a dirty-looking house, but it was somewhere to sleep, and that was all I wanted. A few doors along the street there was an alleyway, where I guessed I would be able to leave the car at night, if I squared someone with a bob or two.

I didn't sleep there that night, because I had to go out to collect my few things, and to let Eggs know about it. But I moved in the following night, and managed to get along to Benny's in time to meet the kid when she came out. She was very surprised to see me, and could hardly believe that I had got myself fixed up already.

"I'm a man about town again," I said.

But it struck me that she wasn't very pleased about it. When I asked her outright, she said she thought it was fine, and she seemed glad that I would be able to see her in the evenings. But all the same she seemed worried about my being back in town, and after we'd had some food at a cafe and I'd walked her home and we'd said good night, she looked up at me and said in a funny sort of way, "Take care of yourself, Bill."

It was two days later when I ran up against Jeff again. I was driving along a street, looking for a certain number where I had to call to see if there was an order. I was crawling along, trying to read the numbers on the houses, and suddenly, about a hundred yards in front of me, I saw Jeff come down the steps of a house and get into a car and drive off. I marked down the house he had come from, and when I got up to it, sure enough it was the number I was looking for.

He was at his little game already. His car was just disappearing round the corner, and I gave chase. He was driving fairly fast, and he'd got a better car than I had, so it was as much as I could do to hang on to his tail. But I couldn't let him get out of sight. This was a duty; this was a part of my job. I shut my eyes for a moment, and there was the kid, and I told her this was my job. I couldn't let Eggs down on this. If the mug thought he could pinch our customers, he was asking for anything that was coming to him.

I drove on, following his car, wondering if to try to head him off while we were still in the town, or to follow him out into the county and give it to him there. But after we had been going for about ten minutes, he answered the question for me by pulling up suddenly.

I drew my car up behind his, surprised at how cool I was feeling. Something told me that I could do this the kid's way. I could do this without getting tough about it. This was a business matter, and it needed dealing with in a business way. The kid would like it more if I did it like that.

As he got out of the car, to go into the house, I jumped out of mine and hailed him. "Hullo, Jeff!" I called.

He spun round as he heard my voice, and when he saw me he looked as if he had seen a ghost. His face went white and his eyes goggled.

"W-What do you want, Bill?" he stammered.

I grinned at him.

"How's business?" I asked.

"Leave me alone," he said.

"Just a minute, Jeff," I said. "Didn't that ducking in the pond do you any good after all?"

"Leave me alone," he said again, and quivered like the gutless mug he was.

"Just a minute," I said to him, walking up and leaning my back against his car. "We've got to understand each other. We're in the same business, you and I, and people in the same business have got to understand each other."

I was playing with him. The kid would have been pleased if she could have heard. The back of his car was full of boxes of eggs, and I put my left hand in and took an egg in my fingers. His eye followed me, so that he didn't notice my right hand stretching across and taking the ignition key out of the dashboard. I slipped the key in my pocket, and then stood there with the egg poised in my fingers. I tossed it gently and then caught it again. "Put that egg down!" he said.

"That's just what I was thinking of doing!" I said, as I tossed it gently up and down. "How many of Mrs. Wharton's customers are you thinking of taking your way?"

He started to splutter. "Mrs. Wharton has never served this house. I got this off my own bat."

I shrugged my shoulders. The weals on my back started to tickle.

I held the egg gently between my fingers, with my arm out at full length. My eyes were fixed on his. Without taking my eyes off his for a moment, I opened my fingers and the egg plopped on the pavement.

"You want to remember," I said to him, "that customers for eggs aren't any good unless you've got eggs for customers."

"What do you think you're doing?" he rasped out. But he wasn't making any move.

"Don't get excited," I told him, "or I'll flatten you out like that egg there."

"You—you—"

As I reached for another egg, he suddenly dived into the front seat of his car and pressed the starter. But the ignition key was safely in my pocket, and the engine only whirred.

"Don't go away before we've finished our little talk," I said, and smiled at him as I tossed the second egg gently up and down in my hand.

"Put that egg down or I'll fetch a policeman!" he said.

I glanced up and down the street. There was nobody about. It was early afternoon and the suburban streets were fairly empty.

"Go and fetch him!" I said. "And tell him about your neat little way of getting business."

He dived out of the other door of the car. "He'll soon stop you!" he shouted, and rushed off up the street and round the corner.

I didn't waste any time. He might be back in a moment with a cop, but he might have to spend quite a few minutes finding one. I banked on the chance of having a few minutes to spare. Leaning over into the back of his car, I lifted up the boxes one by one, and emptied all the eggs out, so that they made a pile on the floor of the car. Then I carefully put a layer of empty boxes on the top of the eggs to keep my feet clean, and then climbed in over the side and stamped. There was a glorious crackling sound as dozens of eggs went. I stamped quickly two or three times until the back of his car was just a mess of yellow and shells. Then, as quickly as I could, I turned my car round in the road and drove off the other way, so as not to meet him coming back.

As I drove along, I thought of the back of that car, and I put my head back and bellowed with laughter.

But the kid didn't laugh about it. I met her on the following Sunday, and when I told her about the trouble with Jeff, she didn't laugh at all. Her face got longer and longer as I went through the story. And when I had finished telling her, she was looking as gloomy as a fog.

"I got away before they came back," I finished.

She nodded her head slowly.

"Yes—this time," she said. "But you can't go on like this. You can't go on with that kind of thing in the streets for long. There's bound to be trouble before long. Why—they're probably on the lookout for you even now!"

I looked at her, puzzled.

"But, kid—I did it your way," I protested. "I didn't slog him. I was as gentle as a lamb with him. Anyone else would have smashed him up for good and all. But I didn't. I could have, easily—but I didn't. Because I wanted to do it your way. Just like a business arrangement."

She smiled for a fraction of a second and then looked serious again.

"I can hardly believe it," she said slowly. "Of all the jobs in the world, one would have thought that this one would steer clear of trouble. But here you are, heading straight for it again already. I can hardly believe it."

"But what are you worrying about?" I asked her. "I've done things in the proper way, haven't I? I couldn't just let him go ahead and pinch all the customers, could I? Besides—we shan't have any more trouble with Jeff. He'll keep clear now he knows he's going to get all his stuff smashed up if he comes near me."

The kid shrugged her shoulders resignedly.

"I'm not really blaming you, Bill," she said. "I admit you couldn't let him go on without doing something to stop him. And I know you did it in the way you thought was best. But it's all a terrible pity." She paused, and then said softly, "Do be careful, Bill. Promise me you'll be careful."

"I've promised you," I said. "You're the only person I've ever promised anything to. Don't worry!"

We were walking along the streets between her room and mine, to pick up the car out of the alleyway. Again it was a warm, brilliant day, and the prospect of rolling gently through the country, lanes with her made everything else seem unimportant. As we climbed into the car and moved out along the streets, I looked round at her sitting beside me and I felt a strange feeling. It was like being one up on everyone else. As we passed people, I looked at them and felt a kind of pity for them. They didn't know her. They weren't sitting beside her. They weren't driving out into the country with her. Not them. Only me. She didn't smile for them. She didn't tell them to be careful, because she didn't care what happened to them. Only me. Just her and me sitting in the car here together, and that put me one up on everyone else.

We went out through the suburbs and soon shook off the town. The country was soft and green. Soon we turned off from the main road to get away from the stream of traffic. I was driving very slowly now, looking round from time to time to have a glance at her. We weren't talking. I was thinking about her, and about me. Three years before, I wouldn't have been here like this—I wouldn't have spent the afternoon with any woman, with any girl. I had never thought twice about anyone, not for as long as I could remember. She was different, but it was hard to say how. Perhaps it wasn't that. Perhaps it was that I was different now. But it was she who had done it to me. No one else ever had, but she had acted on me in a way I wouldn't have believed.

We were right out in the quiet country now. I glanced round at her again. Her lips were slightly apart, and her eyes were dreamy.

I brought the car to a stop on the grass edge by the side of the road. She looked round lazily.

"Don't tell me you've run out of petrol!" She smiled. "It's lovely here, isn't it?"

I nodded. I didn't so much want to talk to her, but I wanted to look at her.

"Let's get out and stretch our legs," I said at last.

"Yes—let's!" she said.

We got out of the car and strolled slowly through an open gate that led into a field. A vague footpath wound its way crookedly from the gate toward the, far side of the field, and there the ground became broken with gorse bushes, like a heath. The sun was softly on our faces, and the quiet country sounds played in our ears. We followed the path. It was narrow, almost too narrow for two, and she kept touching into me, brushing her short-sleeved arm against mine. She walked with easy grace, her head high. She carried her hat in her hand, and the air toyed lightly with a wisp of hair that fell across her forehead.

The footpath led us to a stile, set in a low hedge. I helped her up and over. She was light and lovely, and as I handed her down on the other side, I followed her with one high stride and didn't take my hand away. My fingers were round the soft of her arm, just above the elbow. I could feel the flicker of a tiny nerve, and my hand felt weak and uncertain. We stopped and stood there, hesitating, waiting for something and wondering what it would be.

"Let's sit down on the grass," I said; my voice was strange.

She took her arm away and sat down. Then she let herself fall gently backward, her head on her hands, her elbows out. I dropped down beside her, but the ground was sloping slightly, and as I lay I rolled toward her.

We were very close. Her face was so close that I could see the texture of her skin. I could see the invisible tiny hairs like a bloom on her cheek. Her eyelashes drooped down lazily, her mouth was just apart. The blood in me quickened and warmed. I had kissed her before, just that light, quick once in her room the other night. But my breath was coming quickly now. I moved closer still, so near that she was almost out of focus. Quietly, carefully, I eased my left hand behind her neck and closed it on her shoulders. And then, with a sudden surge, I kissed her mouth. The warmth and the softness of her went into me and through me and I pressed her mouth to mine in a long, fierce clasp.

I felt a hand pressing me up, and she broke away, gasping. "Bill!"

I moved my lips softly across her face, touching her cheeks, her eyes, her tiny ear. My right hand went down to draw her closer to me. It rested on silk. I could feel the tendons in the back of her leg, just above the knee. And then, there wasn't silk any farther.

I felt it coming over me, quick and deep. I pressed my mouth to hers again. With a great uncontrollable wanting I tore at things frenziedly. And suddenly we were together. Suddenly the two of us were melting into one. Suddenly everything dimmed and shook, and everything else in the world had disappeared.

And then, with the warmth of the sunshine and the tiredness of it all, we lay there on the grass and went to sleep.

When I woke up, she was looking at me softly. She was still very close, and I could almost feel her breath playing on my face. She was looking at me softly, carefully, as if she were searching for something.

I shifted my position a bit. The ground was getting rather hard. Her clothes were arranged again as if nothing had happened.

I smiled at her.

"Hullo!" I said.

"Hullo, Bill!" Her voice was very tiny, and she kept her eyes fixed softly on me, searching me all the time.

The fierce wanting was all gone now. It had poured all out of me. And in its place came a funny gentle feeling that I hadn't known before. It wasn't the clammy feeling that you get after a tart. It was something new. It was a curious sense of importance about things, as if something had happened that could not be dismissed just by turning away.

"Are you all right?" I asked her, rather foolishly.

She didn't answer. She just went on looking at me. And then her hand came over and she touched me on the arm, as if to make sure that I was still there.

Gradually, as I watched her, a tear formed in her eye and then trickled down her face, leaving a shining trail.

"What's the matter?" I asked her.

Still she didn't answer. She went on gazing at me, as if she were having some worried kind of dream. And then quite suddenly she said, "Kiss me, Bill!"

I leaned across and kissed her. I thought all the wanting had gushed itself out, but perhaps it hadn't with her.

But it wasn't that. There wasn't any fierceness in it now. She lay there quietly, her lips just apart, and when I took my mouth away she didn't try to hold it there.

"Been to sleep?" I asked her.

"I think so," she said. "Perhaps I still am."

"How do you mean?"

She was silent for a few moments, and then she said, "Why did we do it, Bill?"

I puckered my face.

"Why? Because we felt like it, I suppose."

"Only that? Only because we felt like it?"

"I don't see what you are getting at," I said. "I suppose people only do it because they want to, don't they?"

"Don't talk like that, Bill. Please don't talk like that." Her voice was quivering. "Don't talk about people when you mean you and me. Don't make us sound like everyone else. Not now. Not about that. Please, Bill."

I put my hand on her forehead, and pushed my fingers up gently through her hair.

"You're not like anyone else," I said. "Honest, kid, I've never felt the same about anyone else. You know that."

She nodded her head.

"Yes," she said, "I think I do know that. But it's nice to hear you say it, Bill. I wanted to hear you say it. You see, I never thought I would do that. I've always made my mind up that I wouldn't do that, not before I was married." She smiled. "Do I sound silly?"

It was my turn to search her now. I looked at her with a sudden exultant feeling that I couldn't quite understand. I felt as if I had suddenly become the owner of something, as if something I wanted a lot had suddenly become all mine. I had never thought of her side of it before. There had to be a first time, of course. There had to be a first person. But it had never occurred to me to think about that before. And now, face to face with knowing it for the first time, I found myself feeling glad.

"Then—there's never been anyone else like that with you?"

She shook her head slowly. "I was hoping that you had guessed," she said.

I looked at her and felt a sudden thrill that she was so much mine. I put my arms round her and kissed her, and held her close to me.

"Bill," she said, "you're more important to me now than ever. You've got to keep that promise. You simply must keep it now. I couldn't bear it if things went all wrong again."

"Don't worry," I said, with my arms around her, and all the excitement of her going through me. "Don't worry, kid. Everything is going to be all right. You and me are going to make everything fine!"

On the way back to town in the dusk of the evening, we drove slowly all the way. She was sitting as near as she could to me, and when there wasn't too much traffic, I would let my left hand fall down gently into her lap, feeling the soft separation of her legs. Sometimes I wanted to stop the car, and turn to her and have that time in the field all over again. But we drove on slowly, without stopping, without much talking, remembering it and loving it, and wishing it could happen all the time.

As we got near home, I began to wonder whether there wasn't something special I ought to say. With her, who wasn't like the rest of them, what was the proper thing after doing it the first time? You couldn't just drop it and forget it. But what else? Something told me that she wouldn't want me to suggest that she move into my room. Besides it wasn't big enough or good enough. It wasn't half good enough for her. It wasn't even nearly as good as her own place, and that wasn't half good enough for her now.

I wondered what I ought to say. But while I was puzzling it out, she broke in:

"If you'll drive back to my place, I'll make you a goodnight cup of tea."

"Sounds fine!" I agreed. But then I remembered the time before. I remembered how something had kept butting in between us while we were there. That room made her ask questions. It made us look backward instead of looking forward. There was something about it that reminded us of things. It wasn't any good. I didn't want to go there again. I never wanted to go there anymore.

"No," I said; "suppose you come and inspect my new hideout instead? You haven't seen it yet. There's a gas ring, and tea, and I can rake up a couple of cups. We can have it there, and then I'll run you along home afterward."

"All right," she said. "I'd like to see it. I've been jealous ever since you told me that it only costs twelve shillings a week."

I laughed. "Don't expect too much," I said. "We'll probably find that the mice have been having tea and haven't left any for us."

"Mice? Really?" The kid was horrified. But I told her not to worry.

"They're well trained," I said. "They wouldn't dream of showing up while I have a lady there."

We left the car at the curb outside, and I lighted the way up the stairs by striking matches. The room was on the first floor. I unlocked the door and threw it open. The lights from the street reached up and broke the darkness a bit.

"Here we are," I said.

She went in, and I followed her and shut the door behind me. It was an ordinary lock, and you had to take the key from the outside and lock it again from the inside. When I had done this, I struck another match and lighted the gas jet that jutted out from the wall above the fireplace.

"No electric light? How primitive!" she laughed.

But when the light went up, I saw her face go disappointed. She looked all round the room, her eyes examining everything in turn. She didn't think much of it, that was plain by the way she looked. I began to wish I hadn't brought her in. I began to think that there was something funny about us, so that rooms would always butt in between us, and we would only feel right outside. But she soon smiled.

"It lacks the feminine touch!" she decided. "One of these fine days I'm going to spend a Sunday smartening this place up a bit."

I found her the kettle, and I took it out to the tap on the landing to fill it. When I got back into the room, she had drawn the curtains and put a cloth over the stained table, and already the place looked cozier and brighter.

I lighted the gas ring and put the kettle on, and when it came to the boil she made the tea. We sat over it while we each smoked a couple of cigarettes. Then she put her hand up to her mouth and yawned.

"I can't keep awake much longer." She smiled. "Will you run me home now, Bill?"

"Okay," I said.

We got up from the table, and she walked across to the bed to pick up her hat which she had thrown down on it. I watched her across the room, and to reach the hat she bent forward slightly, so that the back of her skirt drew tight and told about the soft roundness of her. I went over and put my arms round her, and bent to kiss her. I bent still more, so that I could press her to me and feel through her dress where her stockings ended. It was all surging up in me again. Why should she have to go now? What was the point? If you both wanted things, you were meant to have them. Why shouldn't you have them over and over again as quick and as often as you wanted?

I pushed her backward toward the bed, with my mouth on hers. But I felt her struggling, and I took my arms away. She stepped away from me, and looked into my eyes with the same searching look that I had seen when I woke up beside her that afternoon.

"No, Bill," she said. "Not again. Not now." She hesitated, with that same queer kind of worry all over her face. Then she said, "Bill, don't think that I'm—don't think that because of anything that has happened I'm— Oh! I know you don't think so, Bill, but— please take me home now, Bill. I'm so tired."

I looked at her and smiled.

"Come along," I said.

I turned out the light and unlocked the door, and locked it again on the outside, and put the key in my pocket. Then I put one arm round her shoulders, and the other round behind her knees, and lifted her up and carried her down the stairs into the car.

Chapter Nine: BLOOD ON HER HANDS

I wished that I had never let her go. Three nights later, when she came hammering on my door, with all that blood on her hands and that awful horror in her eyes, I could have killed myself for ever letting her go.

For over an hour she couldn't tell the story. For over an hour she just shivered and sobbed, while the weals on my back tickled enough to drive me mad. And when she managed to tell me, it was a slow, jerky story, that tore itself out of her with an effort that hurt to watch.

She had gone home from Benny's in the ordinary way that evening, walking to the first corner with two of the other girls, and then going on alone for the rest of the way. She was nearing the house, when a man who was walking behind her quickened his pace and caught up with her. He bent round and looked into her face carefully, and then touched her arm as if to stop her.

"I want to talk to you," he said.

She looked at him, but he was a stranger. She drew herself away and started to walk on quickly. But he kept up with her, and touched her arm again, and this time he moved right in front of her to bar her way.

"I think you had better talk to me," he said, with a kind of suggestive threat in his voice.

The kid blazed up.

"Leave me alone!" she snapped. "How dare you try to stop me like this!"

She stepped to one side and moved forward, trying to pass him. But before she had taken a couple of steps, he spoke again, in a voice that was quick and sharp.

"It's about Mr. Saunders," he said.

Curiosity got the better of her. She pulled herself up and jerked her head round.

"What?"

He smiled. Looking at him, she saw a man of thirty or so, neatly dressed, with the nastiest pair of shifty eyes she had ever seen.

"It's about Mr. Saunders," he said again. "Or has he given you some other name?"

"I know a Mr. Saunders," said the kid curtly. "What is it you have to say?"

"Something that will interest you very much," he answered.

He had a smooth voice. Too smooth. There was a kind of mocking insolence about it. The kid frowned.

"If you want to say anything to me, say it quickly. I'm in a hurry."

"Plenty of time," he said calmly, taking a cigarette from a case, tapping it carefully, and putting it in his mouth. "You knew, I suppose, that your friend Mr. Saunders was a murderer?"

The blood drained away from her head. She fought to tell herself that she had not heard properly. That awful word. There must be something wrong with her ears.

"What do you mean?" she said. "I don't know what you are talking about!"

"I asked you," he repeated, "if you knew that Mr. Saunders was a murderer. Hasn't he told you about it?"

"Told me about what?" Desperately she tried to clear her mind, to tell herself that this was all nonsense and that this man was just a lunatic.

It couldn't be true. It was a ridiculous thing to say. The man must be drunk. But he was standing there steadily enough, calmly enough. Now he was lighting his cigarette. Now he was shaking the match out and tossing it casually into the gutter. Now he was dragging calmly on his cigarette and puffing out a cloud of smoke.

"I should hate to go into all the vulgar details," he said, "but the police, I am sure, would be very interested to hear all about it." He sighed. "I suppose one day I shall be tempted to tell them. And then you won't be seeing your Mr. Saunders anymore."

She listened, fascinated. There was something about the deliberate attitude of the man that made it seem as if he wasn't fooling. It was just as if he knew he had the upper hand. She wrestled to sort out the thoughts that were tumbling over in her mind. When? How? Who? It couldn't be true. Flitting, hurting, yes—but not murdering, not making somebody die. No. That wasn't true. Nothing would ever make her believe it. It was wicked even to think for a moment that it could be possible. Murder! No. When? Who? No!

"There must be some mistake!" she muttered. "You must be mixing up the name!"

The man smiled. "I'm afraid not," he said. "Much as I wish it were not true, dear lady, I am afraid that it is. Perhaps it would be just as well if I gave you a few of the details, just to convince you that what I say is completely and absolutely accurate."

She stood there in the street, looking at him, hardly daring to listen, yet not daring to run away. He motioned with his hand along the street. "There are better places than this for talking about such private things," he said. "I know where you live, of course. Wouldn't it be better if you invited me in? Then we could talk the whole thing over without fear of anyone overhearing us."

"But I—" The kid hesitated. It couldn't be true. But—just supposing for one fraction of a second that it was. Then she had to know. There must be a mistake. She could put it right, she could get the whole thing straightened out, she could explain what a mistake it all was. But she had to know. When? Who? No, it was all a mistake. But she had to know.

"Very well," she said.

She walked along the street as if in a dream, the man striding beside her.

"It's a nice evening," he said pleasantly.

Her head was going round and she was hardly daring to think. They came to the house, and she let him into the hall, and then unlocked the door of her room and went in. He followed her, taking off his hat with an exaggerated gesture. She shut the door behind him. It was still quite light, but without knowing why, she pulled the heavy curtains across the windows and turned on the light.

"May I sit down?" he asked.

"Please say what you have to say, as quickly as you can," she said.

He sat down on a chair and put his hat on the table.

"It was a long time ago," he said, "but unfortunately that doesn't make very much difference. You would think that sometimes the police would be content to let bygones be bygones. But not they! They are persistent, unforgiving people."

"You mean—you are from the police?"

"Good gracious, no!" He laughed heartily, as if she had made a good joke. "My dear young lady—how you misjudge me!"

"Then—who are you?"

"Who? Oh, just someone who happens to take an interest in you and the murd—I beg your pardon!—you and Mr. Saunders."

"You are simply trying to play some cheap trick on me!"

He shook his head.

"I assure you," he said, "that in my business it would be fatal trying to play tricks on people. I have to deal strictly with the truth. Mr. Saunders—the same Mr. Saunders whom you were with on Sunday, and whom you were with the Sunday before, and with whom, if I may be forgiven for making such a suggestion, you are getting along rather well—killed a man three years ago."

"He didn't! It's not true! I know it's not true!" Her mind was flashing back and counting. Three years. That would be the time.

That would be the night. Just about then. A sudden sinking, deeper than ever, dragged at her and made her heart beat faster.

"This accusation you're making—when was it exactly?"

From his inner breast pocket he pulled a neat little leather notebook and flipped the pages over quickly.

"It was on March the second, to be exact," he said. "Actually three years and a few months ago. At about ten past seven, in the public bar of the Three Crowns in Dane Street."

He looked up from his little book, as if taking a pride in the completeness of his details.

"What date did you say?" she whispered.

"March the second."

That was the night. She had remembered the date, fixing it in her mind as people do with birthdays. That was the night, a Tuesday. The man had died—it had said so in the papers. And she had always known. She had pushed it away and away, but she had always known. Right inside, far back in the darkest hidden corner of her mind, it had been there all the time. But not murder. The man had died, yes, but that didn't mean murder. Every time anyone died, it didn't mean murder. It must have been an accident. A thing like that *could* be an accident....

The man spoke again. "Would you like me to explain things a little more fully?" he asked. "Will you have a cigarette? No? You don't mind if I do? Thank you."

He lit his cigarette and settled himself more comfortably in the chair.

"On that particular evening," he said, "I happened to be having a drink with a friend of mine in the public bar of the Three Crowns. Mr. Saunders was there. Judging from his appearance and condition, he had been there for some little time before I arrived. It is apparently a place where they are accustomed to have—er— trouble now and again, and one of the barmen at the time was a retired pugilist, employed partly for his skill and efficiency in removing people who became a nuisance to the other customers.

"On this particular evening, Mr. Saunders, if you will forgive my saying so, was making himself a considerable nuisance to another customer, having attempted to settle an argument by the simple process of picking up his drink and emptying it into the other man's face."

He paused. The kid stared blindly at him, seeing the scene from his words.

"The barman," the man went on, "was fully capable of dealing with such an incident. In fact, as he came round the bar, my friend—

who was a regular customer there—turned to me with a smile and said, "There he goes," meaning Mr. Saunders. However, Mr. Saunders—as you will probably have noticed yourself—is a man of unusual strength. Moreover, he is a man of the type that does not wait to be hit first. Almost before we knew what was happening there was a crack that went resounding round the whole bar, and the barman was on the floor. Everybody in the room braced themselves up to enjoy what promised to be a really good scrap. But Mr. Saunders had put such incredible force into his blow that the scrap did not materialize. The barman lay quite still on the floor, and after a minute or two we discovered that he was dead."

The words were falling on the kid's ears like dull hammers. "Go on," she whispered.

"There is little more to tell you," the man said. "Mr. Saunders was a wise man. He knew trouble when he saw it, and he didn't wait. He made a dash for it and got away. I myself ventured to join in the chase, but he threw everyone off. It was in the papers the next day, of course, but Mr. Saunders was a stranger in that bar, and nobody seemed to know his name. I imagine the police didn't know whom to look for, so after a while they gave it up as a bad job."

"But *you* knew his name?"

The man shook his head and smiled.

"Not at that time," he said. "I was extremely sorry that I didn't, because in my business it is essential to know names."

"Then—" Desperately the kid clutched at the straw. "How do you know it was him?"

The man waggled his forefinger at her reprovingly.

"Really," he said, "I should hardly be so silly as to pick out someone to fit the situation and then try to pin it on to him. As I have told you before, I always concern myself essentially with facts."

"Then how did you find out? What makes you think that it was him?"

"For a long time," said the man, "I had written the affair off as a dead loss to myself. At first, naturally, I assumed he would be caught. But when they didn't find him, I realized that the incident could be of no practical use to me because I didn't know his name. I could, of course, have given a pretty accurate description of him to the police—the descriptions that were published in the newspapers were hopelessly inaccurate—but I didn't do so because the police and I have never really got on together."

"Then how did you find out his name?"

"In the course of my profession," he explained, "whenever I have nothing better to do, I drop in at the courts so as to keep *au fait* with what is happening on what one would call the irregular side of life. I happened to be doing this three months later, on"—he consulted his little book again—"June the seventh, to be precise. Imagine my surprise when I saw Mr. Saunders in the dock."

"But that was nothing to do with murder."

"Exactly," he agreed. "I realized that the police had not connected the two things together, and that after he had served his term of imprisonment I should be able to enter Mr. Saunders on my list of Open Accounts."

"What do you mean by that?"

"We will come to that very shortly," he said. "Incidentally, I saw you there in the court that day. I was sitting quite close to you. It was a very touching scene, if I may say so. I have kept a casual eye on you ever since, realizing that you would probably be a useful method of keeping in touch with him."

He paused, and lit another cigarette. She had been standing all this time. Now she went over to a chair and sat down. She felt limp and helpless. Everything fitted. It wasn't a mistake. She had always known.

"Are you going to tell the police?"

"My dear young lady, please don't think that I would do anything so thoughtless or unkind. If I had any wish to do that, I could have told them any time after I had seen him in court. No, I want you to look upon me as a friend." He smiled.

"What do you mean? What are you going to do?" she asked.

"Nothing at all," he said. "I am sure that Mr. Saunders is a very charming man. I am sure that you would be very upset if anyone else came to know about this. And so should I."

On the top of all that numb despair came bewilderment.

"But then—what are you—why did you come to tell me this?"

He closed up his little book and put it back into his pocket.

"Business is business," he said. "I have to live, and times are hard. I realize that this is a small matter as far as I am concerned. I know that Mr. Saunders is not earning very much money at present, and that although you have recently had your wages raised, you are still only getting three pounds five per week. I do not believe in being grasping. I have never found that it pays in the long run. I should think, taking everything into consideration, that for the present, until times improve for you both, a pound would be just about right."

"A pound? I don't understand," she said.

"A pound a week," he explained. "I shall give you an address to which it is to be sent."

She gaped at him, an awful fear pulling at her inside.

"You mean you are asking me to pay you money not to tell the police?"

He spread his hands out in a deprecating manner.

"You can hardly call it money," he said. "Why, it is so little, you won't really miss it at all. And think how nice it will be to know that your little secret is in safe hands!"

She thought she was going to faint. She struggled to keep herself sitting upright, to keep herself from screaming, to keep herself from rushing out to get away from him. She had to keep her senses. She had to face this thing without losing her head.

"Why didn't you go to Bill—I mean Mr. Saunders?"

The man shrugged his shoulders. "I thought of doing so," he admitted. "I was very strongly tempted to do so, in the hope that he might be persuaded to steal, and in that way be able to pay more. But in the end I reluctantly decided against it. You see, I have observed Mr. Saunders in action. I realize that he is a powerful man, with possibly a quick temper. If he were to do away with me, it would of course be all the worse for him in the end, but it would not do me any good. No. I know I can rely on you not to tell him about this, because he would almost certainly try to put me out of the way, and in that case he would be hanged. The police wouldn't let him slip twice. So there you are. Remember, the worst thing you can do from your own point of view is to tell him about it."

From his pocket he drew a small piece of paper and a pencil, and started to write.

"This is where to send it," he said. "I shall expect it every Saturday, starting next Saturday. If it does not arrive, the police will be looking for Mr. Saunders by the Monday."

"I won't do it!" said the kid. "I won't do it, I tell you! You daren't do this. You daren't go to the police—they wouldn't believe you!"

He laughed. "You have two or three days to think it over before the first instalment is due," he said. "I usually find that two or three days is enough."

He got up and went to pick up his hat, but hesitated. As she stood there, helpless, watching him, a nasty leer came into his shifty eyes.

"I might, of course, change my mind," he said. "I might decide, when I leave here now, that the right and proper thing for me to do is to tell the police tonight."

She caught her breath. "No!" she gasped. "Please! No!"

She went quickly across the room to him, and caught hold of his arm pleadingly. He looked down at her.

"Sometimes," he said, "in dealing with my more attractive clients, if you will forgive the clumsy compliment, I am encouraged to keep my secret by a little friendliness on their part."

"What do you mean?" she asked.

She had let go of him, and now she moved back a little. He stepped toward her, trying to put his arm around her.

"Mixing business with pleasure is always a good idea," he said silkily.

She pushed him away. "Get out, you filthy beast!" she said.

The smile went. He walked over to the table and picked up his hat.

"Very well," he said. "Mr. Saunders will be arrested before the night is out!"

A sickening chill went down her. A pounding started in her ears. As he moved toward the door, she ran and clutched hold of him.

"No, don't do that—you mustn't do that! I'll do anything you say, but please don't do that!"

He put his arm round her, and this time she didn't dare to move away.

"Don't look so worried," he said softly. "You're far too pretty to worry."

A feeling of sick despair came over her. As her head went spinning round and round, she could only remember that she had to keep this man from telling. He mustn't go out and tell. He mustn't go out until he promised not to tell. There would be some way out later, but she needed time to think. She would be able to sort the thing out as soon as she had time to think. There must be a way. Surely there must be an answer to all this somewhere. But her mind was going round so fast that she couldn't think now. Soon. But she had to have time. Given a little time, she could think of what to do. There must be something to do. But now—keep him here, keep him here. He mustn't go out and tell. He mustn't go out until he promised not to tell.

His arms were closing round her, shutting her in, drowning her. She tried to open her eyes, but she didn't dare look at him. She was hot all over and her heart kept missing.

He put his mouth on hers, and she felt the clammy sucking of his lips. She wanted to retch but she couldn't; it wouldn't quite come. He kissed her again and again, and although her mouth was set and hard, he seemed to find satisfaction in it.

She let him go on. If he liked it, let him do it. If this would stop him from telling, it was worth all the feeling of muck and filth that it gave her.

He took his mouth away from hers, and stroked her forehead, fondled her hair. Now, free to breathe again, her head started to clear a little. She must play up to him. She must make herself out to be friendly, if that was what he wanted. She must make him pleased with her. The thing to do was to keep him from getting cross, to make him go away pleased with her, so that he wouldn't tell. And then, when he had gone, she would have time to think, and be able to sort out what was the best thing to do.

She must play up to him. Get friendly. That was the way to gain time.

She forced herself to smile.

"Gracious!" she said. "You squeezed me so hard you took my breath away!"

That was the way. Be friendly. She had to play him at his own game. She had to keep a clear head, and pretend about everything.

He let go of her and stood away, his leering eyes enjoying the look of her.

"That's more like it!" he said. "You're prettier than ever when you smile."

He sat down on the edge of the bed and lighted another cigarette. Apparently he was not in any hurry.

She made her face smile again. This was the way. It was working splendidly. He had dropped that threatening attitude, and was friendlier now. She sat down on a chair, deliberately casual.

"Let me see—I have that address you gave me, haven't I? Yes, here it is. Well"—she glanced at the clock—"isn't it getting late!"

With his hand he patted the bed beside him, in a kind of invitation to her to go and sit there.

"There was no hurry," he said. "We were just beginning to get along nicely."

"But I'm frightfully tired, really." She had to get him out of the room while they were still friendly. Then he wouldn't tell—not yet, anyway. He would wait for the money, the way he had said in the first place. It was just that he must not be annoyed. She had to get him out while they were still friendly. Now.

She got up and went over to him, crushing down the loathing, making a tremendous effort to smile. She took hold of his hands and tried to pull him up to his feet.

"Come on," she coaxed.

He sat there, his hands in hers, looking up and down her. Then he fixed his eyes on hers. He tightened his hands, so that now she was not holding his but he was holding hers. Slowly, gradually, she felt herself being pulled nearer to him. Her hands were right close to his chest now, so that she was having to bend forward. She was almost off her balance. Suddenly, with a quick twist, he let go of one of her hands and jerked the other toward him, so that she could not help herself from turning half round and falling across the bed by his side. As she fell, his free arm came over and held her there.

He bent his face down toward hers. Her head was spinning again. She tried to sit up, but his arm was holding her down. She wanted to scream, but she dared not. Her head was going round, and all she could remember was that she had to keep him from telling.

She felt him turning her. She felt him move over, so that now her body was held down by his. The ceiling was blurred, and she didn't know why she was lying there, why she was letting this man sprawl over her, except that she had to stop him from telling and that was all that mattered.

His hands were crawling over her like lice. Where were they going now? No! O, please God, no! Not there! He couldn't do that. He mustn't tell. He must keep his hands away from there, but he mustn't be made to tell. The only thing that mattered was that he mustn't tell. Nothing else mattered. It was only his hands; that was better than having him tell. He mustn't tell.

In a blind despair she felt him taking hold of her. Desperately she wriggled herself free and broke away from him, pushing herself up from the bed and almost jumping to the other side of the room. There she stood panting, terrified, waiting for him to come at her.

But he didn't get up. He stayed there, lying on the bed, his eyes cruelly enjoying her. Then he turned his head away, and lay on his back looking up at the ceiling, waiting.

"You had better come back to me," he said. "I have told you what will happen if you don't."

Suddenly she saw him clearly. She saw him as something that stretched across her future years like an endless pain. She saw him as a crawling slug, something only fit to be trodden on and squashed out on the pavement. Her small hands clenched in desperate fury. All she knew now was a big, blind hating of him. In a passionate spasm of frenzy she turned round quickly to the shelf behind her, and picked up the first thing that came to her hand. It was a wire toasting fork. Gripping it tightly, she rushed across the room and struck at him blindly.

It was a puny weapon against him, and would hardly have gone through his waistcoat. But just as she brought it down, he turned his head and saw her, and brought up his hands quickly to protect himself. His hands caught the stiff wire handle and pushed it upward, away from his chest. But he wasn't quick enough to stop it. He only altered its course. It came down with all the strength that terror gave her, and the prongs went straight into his throat. As he felt the stab of pain he tried to scream, but it changed into a gurgling cough. A spurt of blood came out of his neck, while the fork fell sagging down, still held by his flesh. His eyes were staring, as she watched him struggle up to a sitting position on the side of the bed. His tie and his collar were all red. His fingers were pawing at his throat, and his face was working horribly. He tried to get up, but he swayed and went down onto the floor. The whispering gurgle was coming from him all the time, as with one hand clutched to his throat he tried to crawl across the floor.

For a moment she stood there watching him, stiff and unable to move. And then, white-faced and taut, she rushed for the door and went through it and slammed it behind her, and went through the outer door and ran blindly through the streets.

Chapter Ten: A CLOSE CALL

She sat shivering in my room, with her eyes fixed straight in front of her.

"Did anyone see you come here?"

She couldn't answer any questions. I put my arm round her and tried to soothe her. I filled the basin with water, and washed her hands, and then took it and emptied it carefully down the lavatory, pulling the plug on it twice to make sure that there was none of the pink color left. Then I made her some tea. She didn't want to drink it, but I held the cup to her lips and forced it into her mouth. After a time she stopped shivering, and gradually some of the fixed look went out of her eyes.

"Did anyone see you come here?"

"I don't know. I didn't look. I just ran."

There were people in the street outside, but they were only walking by, and there didn't seem to be anyone taking a particular interest in the house. I leaned right out of the window to see the dock up the street. It was just after eleven. She had been here getting on for two hours, and she was steadier now. It ought to be safe to leave her for a little while.

"Just sit here quietly," I said to her, "and don't go out of the room. Whatever you do, don't go outside of this room until I get back. I shan't be long."

"Where are you going?" The toneless voice was hardly hers at all.

"Just out. I want to walk and think for a bit. Don't worry. Leave everything to me. Just sit here quietly and wait till I get back."

She looked at me as if she hardly knew me. "Don't leave me alone," she said.

"I must. Just for a little while. I won't be long. Just promise me you'll sit here quietly."

She didn't answer. I looked around for her handbag, but she hadn't got one. She might have the key of her room in her pocket, but I did not dare to ask her, because she might want me to explain.

I went out of the room, and locked the door quietly behind me. Then I went down into the street, and walked swiftly in the direction of her room. I wished I had her key, but if necessary I would have to find a way of getting in without it. If the man was not dead, I had got to kill him. There was no doubt about that, no choice at all. He would be hanging like a black cloud over both of us for always.

He would suck us till we starved.

The kid didn't know. The blood and the gurgling whisper and the stare in his eyes were all she knew. He might have been dying when she left, or he might not. I had to know.

I walked quickly, not running because I did not want to draw any attention to myself. How I was going to get into the kid's room without the key I hadn't yet decided.

But I need not have worried about that. As I came round the corner, into sight of her house, I pulled up short. There were people standing in the street outside the house, about a dozen or twenty of them. They were not in a crowd, but in separate groups of two or three, like the last remnants of a crowd that has mostly moved away. They were talking together, and looking at the house, and one of them kept pointing as if to explain something.

I went on again, getting nearer to them. The curtains were drawn across the windows of the kid's room, but a gap showed that the light was still on. I slowed down my pace to a saunter, and as I drew level with the house, with the people grouped round me, I paused and put a cigarette into my mouth.

"Got a match?"

The man I asked nodded, and brought out a box and struck one for me. Then he seemed to realize that I was a new arrival on the scene, and eagerly started to pour out the news.

"Hear about the murder?"

I tried to keep my face in the shadow, just in case.

"Murder?"

"Yes—they just took the body away in an ambulance. Wasn't half a gory one, too, they say. It was covered up when they brought it out, but the old landlady was fair screaming her head off when she found it."

"Where did it happen?"

"In this house here. The landlady found the body in the hall. She reckons he'd crawled out of a room on the ground floor and then pegged out. A girl did it, they say. At least, it was a girl's room where it was done in, so it was probably her that did it."

"He didn't say?"

The man looked at me pityingly.

"How can you say when you're dead?" he asked.

I muttered something and moved on. So he was dead when they found him. He didn't do any telling first. But what difference did that make? They would be looking for the kid. At this very moment they would be looking for the kid.

What I had to do was keep my head and think straight. Unless she had been followed—and that seemed out of the question, because they would have burst in on us before I left there—then it did not seem likely that the police would trail her to me. I had only had my new room a couple of weeks. The kid's landlady had never seen me. If it had been me they were trailing, they would have watched her straight away, because the prison record would have told them that she came to see me there. But that didn't work the other way round. She had no record. They would not check back on her that way. I couldn't see why they should trail her to me. They had got no starting point. Benny's would be their first kickoff, and that would not lead to me. Nobody at Benny's knew my name, and nobody would remember or connect up that one time when I barged in there to see her.

The police would be at work already, but they wouldn't get far tonight. The landlady would tell them where the kid worked, and what time she usually arrived home. But when it came to the questions about her men friends, and who came to see her in her room, and whether the dead man was a frequent visitor, then they would start drawing blank.

Somebody might have seen the kid dash out of the house, but unless they had followed her up, that would not help. They had nothing that would lead to me. While she stayed in my room and kept out of sight, she was as well-hidden as she would be anywhere. Short of searching house-to-house over the whole town, there was no reason why they should look for her there.

They would check up at Benny's tomorrow, but her friends there did not know me. Even if they had seen me with her, there was no reason why they would have taken any special notice of the fact.

They would check up on the hotels, and try to find whom she knew well enough to go and ask for hiding. They would look for relations, but the kid was pretty well alone in the world from the family point of view. There might be an odd cousin or something somewhere

I pulled up sharply in the middle of my stride. I had suddenly remembered Eggs.

They would try to trace the kid through her. They would go out to the chicken farm to see if the kid was hiding there. When they started asking questions, Eggs would tell them about me as being a special friend of the kid's, and in a flash they would have the whole thing lined up. I didn't think Eggs had the address of my room, but she was sure to let out that I had charge of her car. At this very minute the car was standing in an alleyway only a hundred yards away from where the kid was. It would bring the search so near that I might as well have had a flag hanging out of the window.

I went stone cold. For the first time in my life I was plain frightened. If it had been me, I could have made a run for it. But being the kid, it was different. If only she could lie low in my room until things had cooled down a bit, then I would be able to smuggle her right out of town to somewhere miles away, where nobody would know her, and she could change to being somebody else. But I did not want to risk it yet. A man can get by with these things better than a girl. I did not want to risk her out of that room until the first shouts of the chase had died down. Yet, through Eggs and the car, they might come smelling us out if we stayed there.

With my back beginning to tickle, I walked on quickly toward my room. How soon they would get on to Eggs it was impossible to guess. They might wait to check up the local things first. They might even never try the farm at all. You couldn't tell. Sometimes, when they knew whom they were looking for, they tried everything they could think of while it was hot.

I reached the house, and ran up the stairs into my room. The kid was lying on the bed, and her face was wet with crying.

I went over and sat on the edge of the bed, and put my arm around her shoulders. At the sight of her face, drawn with misery, I knew that all my life I would kill anyone who ever laid a finger on her.

"Thank heaven you're back, Bill," she whispered. "I began to think you were never coming."

I held her with my arm, and stroked her hair. I wished I could stay with her, never leaving her for a moment, but I had to get going. I had to keep my head and not waste time. Minutes might be counting.

"Listen, kid," I said, as gently as I could. "We've got to talk a bit. We've got to make sure that nobody finds you here. Now just try to think for a minute. Would there be anything in your room that could possibly connect you up with your aunt?"

She spoke as if she had not heard me.

"I wonder if I killed him? I wonder if I killed him?"

I shook her gently.

"Listen! It's very important that you should tell me this. Please try to think. Was there any trace of your aunt's name or address in your room?"

She heard this time. She turned her head and looked at me, as if bewildered to think that anything like that could matter at a time like this.

"There might have been a letter. There probably was."

Her voice was flat and toneless, but the words sizzled in my ears like a time fuse. If there was a letter, then Eggs might be the very first clue they followed up. I had to make an effort to get to her first, and I had to get that car away at once, before they started looking for it.

I went to the window. It was just after midnight, and there was nobody much about in the street. I turned to the kid.

"I've got to leave you again," I said. "It may be several hours, I'm afraid. I can't help it. I've got to try to make certain that they won't find you here. I've got to go and warn your aunt not to tell anybody."

From the way she looked at me, I could tell that she did not properly understand what it was all about. Her head was not really clear yet. But she didn't start any questions.

"Don't let them arrest me for it, Bill" she said, with her lips all quivering. "Please don't let them arrest me for it."

I smiled, and tried to look as if there was nothing to worry about. "Just you stay right inside this room and keep quiet," I said. "We'll soon have everything all right. But whatever you do, don't go outside this room. In fact, I'm going to lock you in, just for safety."

She wanted to go along the landing. I listened at the door, but the house was quiet.

"It's the far door along to the left," I whispered. "I'll go first to make sure it's all clear. Then, when you want to come back, give two soft taps on the door. Then listen. If it's still all clear, I'll tap the landing window twice. Don't come out till you hear me tap, and then come back here as quickly as you can."

I went along, and it was empty. As I waited for her to come out again, my heart was thumping so loudly that for a moment I thought it was somebody coming upstairs. But it was all right. The two little taps, then my soft taps on the window, and she was safely back in the room again.

I locked her in, and went out and along the street to the alleyway. I walked as quietly as I could, putting my feet down toe first, to avoid the clatter of my heels on the pavement, looking into the shadows, turning my head to search every way. The street was deserted except for a man and a woman slouching wearily home, but not a single darkened doorway could be trusted. As I got to the opening of the alleyway I slid into the door of a shop on the other side of the street, and stood listening and peering down toward where the car was. There might be somebody in the alleyway, a couple with nowhere to go, or even a copper doing his rounds. Starting the car up at this time of night would not arouse any suspicion in itself, but if questions were asked afterward, anybody who saw me might check back with their mind and start remembering. The closeness of that car to my room was a possible source of danger, a very big danger if things went wrong, and I could not take the slightest extra risk.

After standing there for a couple of minutes, not seeing or hearing anybody, I slipped quietly across the street and down the alleyway. The car was already facing the right way to go out. I lifted the bonnet and flooded the carburetor, in the hope of making the engine start first go. Then I got into the driving-seat, turned on the switch, and pressed the starter. The moment the engine fired I put her into gear and got her out of the alleyway as quickly as I could, not switching on the lights until I had swung round into the street.

The starting up and getting away had only taken me a few seconds, and it was very unlikely that anyone had seen me go. There was practically no traffic about, and I was through the outer suburbs in half the time it usually took. I should be at the farm within the hour. That would make it a little after one o'clock. The village would be sound asleep, and so would Eggs. She would have been in bed for hours. It was difficult to decide how much I ought to tell her, but I would have to tell her enough to make her realize the importance of keeping her mouth shut. There was, of course, a chance that she might not be willing to help cover the kid up. She might be so shocked about it that she would not agree to have any hand in the thing at all. But that was a chance that simply had to be taken. I was banking everything on her affection for the kid. I knew she was very fond of her, and that would probably make her eager to believe that there must be some excuse for what had happened. Anyway, it had to be tried. There was everything to be gained, and hardly anything to be lost.

There was a big moon now, and it was lighting up the road and the hedges so that as I approached the village I was able to turn the headlights off. This was a good thing, because the beam might have flashed in through some cottage windows and wakened the people up, and the arrival of a car there at this time of night was unusual enough to start the villagers gabbling. I went through slowly on top gear, so as to make as little noise as possible, and when I turned up the lane that led along to the farm, I put the sidelights and the rear light out as well, in case anybody in the village should be awake and see me from their windows.

When I reached the farm, I swung the car into the yard and turned the engine off. The dog started kicking up a furious din, but I called out to him, and as soon as he heard my voice he stopped barking and came up to me. I walked across to the front door and was just about to knock on it, when the window above opened, and Eggs's head came out. The dog had wakened her.

"Who's there?"

I stepped back from the door and called up to her.

"It's me—Bill Saunders! I've got to talk to you. It's very important."

She peered down and saw me.

"Gracious! Whatever are you doing at this hour? Do you know what time it is?"

"I'm sorry, but I've got to talk to you. I couldn't leave it till the morning. It's very important, do you understand? Will you come down and let me in?"

She looked down at me for a moment as if checking up that I was sober. But she was a sensible woman, and as soon as she realized I was serious, she drew her head back into the room, and after a minute I heard her shuffling down the stairs in her slippers. She opened the door, with a candle flickering in her hand.

"Come in! What is it? Is something wrong?"

I went in, not quite knowing how to start. She led the way into the parlor, and lighted the lamp on the table. In that house, set right on its own with the fields all round it, it was quiet, almost eerie, as we stood there. By the light of the oil lamp I could see the puzzled expression on her face. I sat down on a chair.

"It's about the kid—Jane," I started.

"Is she ill?"

I shook my head.

"It's difficult to know how to start," I said. "She's in a jam."

"In trouble?"

"Yes. Bad trouble. And you can help her, in a way."

"Well, tell me what it is," she said. "Don't keep me on edge like this. Of course I'll do anything I possibly can."

I hesitated. "It's not easy to explain, Mrs. Wharton. It's going to be hard for you to understand."

"Don't talk in riddles!" she said impatiently.

I shrugged my shoulders: She had to know. "The police are looking for her," I said.

Just for a moment she looked horrified. But then the practical side of her came out on top. "What do they want her for? What do they imagine she has done?"

She might as well know it all. If we were going to get her help, it was better to tell her everything at the beginning than let her find it out from someone else.

"They want to arrest her for killing someone," I said slowly.

"*Killing* someone?" The way she said it, I almost stopped believing it myself.

"Yes, killing someone," I repeated. "She has killed someone, and naturally they will want to take her for it."

"But—is it a mistake? You don't mean she has really killed someone?"

I nodded.

"That's what I mean," I said.

"By accident?"

"Not exactly. In fact, the police won't look on it as an accident at all. They are much more likely to call it murder."

As I used the word, the color went right out of her face. She put her hand out and took hold of the mantelpiece, as if to stop herself from swaying. Then she sat down on a chair and stared at me. Gradually she pulled herself together, and then said in a firm voice, "Tell me all about it."

"I can't exactly tell you about it," I said. "But the point is that it wasn't the kid's fault. I know it wasn't her fault, and I want you to believe that too."

Anxiously, I waited for her answer. It came quickly and unhesitatingly; "Of course it wasn't! It couldn't be! I know her too well for that. But tell me about it. Where did it happen? When did it happen?"

"It happened a few hours ago, that's all," I said. "It was in her own room."

"Where is she now?"

"She's safe for the present," I answered, dodging the question.

"How did it happen?"

"I'd rather not explain it all now," I said. "I want to get back as quickly as possible. The reason I came straight on here tonight was because I wanted to put you on your guard."

"On my guard? Against what?"

"It's just possible that the police may come and ask you questions. And it's possible that they will come very soon—perhaps tomorrow, perhaps even tonight. You see, they'll be looking for her, and they may think she's hiding here."

"But she isn't."

"No—but they'll try to see if they can get information out of you that will help them to find out where she is. That's where you'll need to be on your guard."

"But I don't follow. I don't even know where she is myself."

"I know that," I said, "but I'm going to get her out of this jam, so I don't want them following me up either. They'll ask you all sorts of questions. When did you see her last? You say that she came out to see you a couple of weeks ago. Did she come alone? You say yes. Has she any men friends that you know of? You say no. That's the important thing to remember—don't mention anything about me at all. They mustn't know that the kid and I have ever even seen each other, or they may try to trace her through me."

"But how could they?"

I shrugged my shoulders. "I can't go into all that now. You'll just have to take my word for it. Please—if you've got any faith in the kid and want to help her—take my word for it and don't breathe a word about me and her."

I stood up and moved toward the door.

"I must get back," I said. "I'm leaving the car here. If I keep it anywhere near me in town it might give them a clue. You never know. I'm afraid you'll have to manage without me for a bit."

She put out her hand as if to stop me.

"Do tell me some more," she said. "What is going to happen? What made her do it? They are bound to find her in the end, aren't they? Oh, this is a terrible, unbelievable thing!"

She was looking so upset that I went across to her and put my hand on her shoulder for a moment.

"Let's hope for the best," I said. "I'll find some way out of it all."

I opened the front door and put on my hat. "Goodbye," I said. "And remember—if the police do come and see you—be on your guard every time you open your mouth."

"You're not taking the car? How are you going to get to town?"

"I'll manage," I said. "Good night."

"Here—wait a moment!" She called me back from the door. "I won't keep you more than a couple of seconds."

She hurried up the stairs, and came down again carrying some money in her hand. She held it out to me.

"Take this," she said. "It is all I have here, but it may help. If she needs money, remember I have nearly a hundred pounds saved up in the bank."

I took the money and stuffed it into a pocket. "Thanks," I muttered, as I turned and went into the lane and started walking quickly toward the village.

I was planning to jump a night-transport lorry as soon as I reached the main road. But I had not gone far when I suddenly stiffened, and then dived into the hedge at the side of the lane. The lights of a car were coming along from the direction of the village. I pressed myself into the hedge to keep the headlights from shining on me, and as the car went past I strained my eyes in the moonlight to see who was inside.

There were two blue-hatted coppers. It was barely five minutes since I had left the farm. If the police had come while I was in there talking, it might have finished everything. As it was, if they found Eggs up in the middle of the night like this, they would take a bit of shaking off. I started to run back along the lane toward the farm, until I came in sight of the house. The police car was standing in the lane outside, and my hopes jumped up when I saw there were no lights showing in the windows of the house. Eggs must have gone straight back to bed. By a matter of minutes, perhaps by seconds, those coppers had missed seeing lights in the house as they drove up.

I tiptoed on along the lane until I was only about fifty yards away. I didn't dare go any nearer. I could vaguely hear the sound of voices, but I couldn't catch what anyone was saying.

Then there was the flickering light of a candle in the room upstairs, and then it was at the open door, and then it was in the parlor, and after a few seconds the brighter light of the oil lamp came.

I stood there waiting, wishing I could go along and help Eggs play her part. But what I had to do was to keep myself out of sight. About a quarter of an hour went by, and then the light went upstairs again, and appeared first at one front window and then at another. The car was still outside the house. They were clearly searching the place, making sure that the kid hadn't got out here somehow, and was hiding. That was all right; they would draw a blank. I wondered if they would search the outhouses, and with a sudden jump I remembered that I had left the car near the side of the house in the yard. If they noticed it and examined it, they would find the engine still warm.

Helpless, I stood there straining my eyes to try and see what was happening. But it looked as if they were satisfied. The light came downstairs, hovered at the door, and then I could hear the sound of their engine starting up again. The car backed into the yard, and then nosed forward toward the village again. I dropped into the ditch by the side of the road just in time to avoid the headlights as they swept round. The car went past me again, and I watched the lights twist along the lane and disappear.

I looked back at the house. The light was up in Eggs's window again now. I wanted to go back and hear what they had said to her, and what she had told them. But I guessed, by the fact that the coppers had gone, that she had done her part well, and I wanted to get back as soon as I could to make sure that the kid was all right. I couldn't do any more good with Eggs. Either she had done all right or else it was too late.

I turned on my heel and strode off quickly in the direction of the village. Approaching it, I cut off through a gate across the fields, skirting around the back of the village to avoid walking through it and risking being heard. I came out on the road again beyond the village, and walked for nearly an hour. Once or twice I had to duck into the hedges as the lights of cars came flashing along the road. At last, as I crouched in the hedge for another pair of lights, I realized that they were coming very slowly, and as they got near I could hear the rattling trundle of a heavy lorry.

I waited until it was just abreast of me, and then I jumped out of the hedge and ran out into the road after it, and found a handhold and hoisted myself aboard. Half an hour later, as we rattled through the suburbs, I dropped off into the road and started walking again. It was nearly four o'clock by the time I dragged myself upstairs to the door of my room.

I opened the door and tiptoed in and locked the door behind me. As I listened I could hear a steady breathing. I struck a match, and by the light of it I could see the kid lying on the bed. She was still in her clothes, but fast asleep. I blew out the match, and keeping as quiet as I could, I curled myself up on the floor without even troubling to take my shoes off. I remembered the last time I had slept on the floor, with the kid fully dressed on the bed. That time it was me. This time it was her. That time it hadn't mattered, but this time it was her.

The daylight was creeping through the curtains by the time I got to sleep.

Chapter Eleven: YOU CAN CHANGE SOME THINGS

I slept for less than two hours, and when I awoke the kid was still asleep. She must have been tired right out by it all, and I was glad she was getting some proper rest. Our plans had to be laid very carefully. I felt sure that Eggs had not let us down, and now that she was on her guard and the car was well away from the district, I could not see that there was any reason to fear that the kid would be trailed here. I went through all the angles of it in my mind, over and over again, and decided that it would be an absolute outside chance if anything cropped up to lead them here.

She was safe for the time being, as long as we could keep her presence in my room a secret. I had no idea at all who the other occupants of the house were, but it was probably let out for the most part in single rooms like mine, and it was not the kind of place where people took very much interest in neighbors. Nobody would come into my room in the ordinary way. I had always kept it locked, and although the owner would probably have a passkey to all the rooms, there was a bolt on the inside of the door which the kid could fasten. The important thing was for her to keep quiet, so that nobody would tumble to the fact that there was anyone else in my room. We would have to keep our voices soft when we talked, and she would have to stay well clear of the window.

She would not be able to hide here indefinitely. As soon as possible, as soon as the hubbub had died down a bit, I would get her right away. That would not be easy, but I could manage it all right. I might get her out into the country, miles away, where she would never be suspected. I might get her out of England altogether, over to Canada on a tramp steamer. That would need to be worked out very carefully, but as long as she kept well clear of any friends or relations, or any place where she had ever been known before, the odds were against her ever being picked up. The police either got you while the trail was warm, or else they nabbed you as soon as you picked up some old connections. They hardly ever got you any other way. The great thing was not to get on the run. If you got on the run, you aroused suspicion everywhere.

With ordinary luck she would be all right here for at least a fortnight. By that time I would have made our plans completely, and we would both disappear for good.

I fetched some water, and as quietly as possible I had a bit of a wash. She was still sleeping when I had finished, and I put the kettle on and sat on a chair smoking cigarettes, waiting for her to wake up, and thinking what a mess I had got her into. Here she was, wanted for killing, the kind of person who would not willingly have hurt a mouse. And it was all because of me; it was all my fault. It would never have happened except for me. She did it because of me. Yes, by God! There was no arguing out of that. She did it because of me. All right; then what happened from now on was up to me too. We were in it together now. It was both of us or none of us. Let them come for her, let them try to take her, and I would kill them and go on killing them as long as there was anything left in me.

She was stirring now. As she turned her head over and opened her eyes, gradually seeing the room and wondering about it, remembering, and all the worry coming back into her eyes, still that queer little curve of her mouth made you think that she was just going to smile, until you looked up again into her eyes and saw that all the fun had gone.

She looked at me in silence. Then she looked at the door, and the window, and all round the room, and quickly over her shoulder at the wall behind her. Then her hand went up to her throat for a second.

"What is going to happen?"

Her voice was tight and jerky. I stood up and turned toward the kettle.

"What is going to happen is that you're going to have a cup of tea," I said.

"No, Bill. I must go and—oh, I don't know what I ought to do, but I must do something!"

"Try and ease up, kid," I said. "You're not going to do anything just at the moment except sit where you are and have a cup of tea."

I filled the teapot and poured out two cups, and took one of them over to the bed and held it out to her.

"Here you are—drink it!" I said.

She took the saucer in her hand, and balanced it on the bedclothes. Then I put a cigarette into her mouth and held a match for her. Together we sipped our tea and smoked in silence for a while.

"I wonder if I killed him," she said at last.

It was no good keeping her in the dark about it.

"You did," I said.

The hand that was holding her cup jerked a little, but her voice was strangely steady as she said, "Why do I feel so cold and collected? How can I kill someone and then feel so calm about it?"

That's the way it sets in sometimes. I hoped it would last.

"It's the best way to feel," I said. "If you can keep yourself from going off the end, we've got twice the chance."

"Twice the chance of what?"

"Getting away."

She shook her head.

"I can't get away," she said, in a dead, matter-of-fact tone. "How can I get away? They will arrest me for it. They are bound to find me soon, and then they will put me in prison for it—or hang me for it."

"They wouldn't do that," I said quickly. "They don't hang you for killing slugs like that. If you told them what happened, they wouldn't think of hanging you; they wouldn't even put you in prison for very long. They might even let you off." I thought for a second or two, and then said, "It might be the best way—to give yourself up. You'd be taking a chance on what they did; but if you don't, you'll be taking. a bigger chance in getting away. It might be the best way; kid. Give yourself up and tell them everything."

We were looking straight at each other. I knew what it meant, and so did she.

"You know I couldn't do that, Bill. If I started to tell them anything, I would have to tell it all. And that would mean giving you away." She shook her head. "No—even if they catch me, I can't tell them. That's obvious."

She said it as if there were no alternative. I looked at her questioningly.

"But I got you into it all," I said. "You mustn't worry about me. Why should you? It's up to you to do what's best for yourself."

She shook her head firmly.

"I couldn't do that," she said again. "I should lose everything in the world if I did that." Suddenly the deliberate manner left her, and she clenched her hands and trembled.

"Bill—I daren't get caught! I must hide somewhere! Do you think—do you think it is possible to escape?"

"It's not only possible—we're going to do it," I said. "If we're in it together, you and I can do anything!"

"But won't they come for me? Shouldn't we run away now, at once, quickly? Isn't it silly to be staying here like this? Surely they will find me here!"

"No, I don't think so," I said. "The great thing is not to get on the run. I've been thinking the thing out carefully. I don't believe they'll trace you here at all, and in that case the best plan is for you to stay hidden in here for at least a week, while the excitement dies down a bit. By that time I'll have everything mapped out, and before you know where you are you'll be miles away, where nobody knows you, where nobody will ever find you. Leave it all to me, kid. Please leave it all to me."

She looked at me softly now, trustingly. Even her eyes did not say anything about it being my fault.

I went down into the street to get a paper, to see the kind of way it was shaping up. The kid was splendid. She had hold of herself like a man, and it was going to make things a lot easier. If I'd had a screaming, sniveling woman to handle, it would have been hell. But she was good, and now I was stone cold too, and that was the best way to be for both of us. We had a chance that way.

I walked a couple of streets, so as to get to a paper shop where I had not been before. It was later than my usual time for going out, and I did not want to draw even that amount of attention to myself. I passed the alleyway quickly, hoping that there had not been any notice taken of the fact that the car was not there anymore. They would simply think I had gone out early, and when the evening came and the car did not show up again, they would only think—if they thought at all—that I had found a better place to put it. There was nothing to worry about there. There was nobody loafing about the street, and I was sure the house was not being watched.

I found a paper shop, and bought three different papers. I tucked them casually under my arm, and strolled out of the shop. I was meaning to take them back to the room and study them carefully there, but I had not gone very far along the street before the desire to see what they said got the better of me. I stopped, unfolded one of them, and ran my eye over the front page. There was no mention of it there, so I turned the paper open at the center spread, where they put the next most important news.

There was no need to search. Something hit me in the face, sending the blood right down into my toes and starting the weals on my back tickling like mad. I stood still in the street, gaping at it, wanting to put my fist straight through the middle of that sheet of paper. It was something I had not counted on, something that had never entered my head, and it squashed into pulp all my cocky ideas about getting the kid away to safety.

In the middle of the page was a big photograph looking out at me with soft eyes, nose tilted, and a twist of the mouth that made it look as if she was just about to smile. *The Police Want to Interview This Girl.*

I gaped at it, with my heart pounding, and the fury rising in me.

So they wanted to interview her, did they? Just like that, just nice and pleasant like that. The hell they did!

I had her, I could keep her safe, out of the way of every prying dick. But for how long? She could not stay forever in my room. I could have got her away, right away off the map, where nobody knew her and nobody ever would—but not now. Not with this damned photograph. This few square inches of paper had bitched the whole thing. Now the whole blasted place was full of amateur detectives. Now every snooping fool in the country would be peering at all the faces he could find. Now there was not a town, not even a village, where she was not half known already.

They must have found this photograph in her room, and splashed it into the papers in the hope of getting her spotted while she was on the run. But it did not end there. This was just the kind of thing the busybodies liked. For weeks, for months, even for years, people would be trying to remember her face, trying to find it, keeping their eyes open for every stranger. That kind of thing in a daily paper did not die at the end of the day. For ages that photograph might be part of the tablecloth in thousands of homes. It might be showing on parcels under women's arms. We would never know. Wherever she went, it would be hanging over her head for years, forever.

A trapped, stifling feeling came over me. I wanted to fight for her, but I didn't know how. Nothing could stop the people from seeing that photograph. And if they saw it, and then saw her, it was likely as not that they would recognize her. She had a face that was easy to remember, and this photograph was just the dead spit of her.

I looked through the other two papers that I had bought, and they both had it. There were long accounts of the affair, too, but they would not have mattered without the picture. The reports themselves did not give much of a line on the kid. But they all had the photograph. Millions of people were vaguely looking for her face.

I bunched up the papers and chucked them over the railings into an area. It was no good taking them back and letting the kid see them. They would shake her into a funk if anything would.

I went and bought a stock of food—cold meat, Ryvita, fruit, and some tinned stuff. She had to eat, and it would help her to keep from getting jumpy. At present she was having a reaction after the shock, but at any time that might wear off, and then she would probably be a handful. It was better for her not to know about that photograph yet. It reduced our chances terribly, and it would make me sound just like a windbag when I told her I could get her away all right. If we were going to beat this jam now, I would have to think pretty hard and pretty fast. But the two great things were to keep my head clear and to keep the kid from rocking.

Back in the room, she was standing looking out of the window, searching the street. I dropped my parcels on the table, and grabbed her by the wrist and pulled her quickly back.

"Don't be a fool!" I snapped at her. "Didn't I tell you to keep away from the window?"

"But Bill—no one knows me in this street. Besides, the only people who could possibly see me would be the people in the rooms across the way. And I'm sure *they* don't know me."

"Everybody knows you!" I said, without thinking what I was saying. But she picked the words up quickly.

"What do you mean—everybody knows me?"

I tried to cover up.

"I mean it's safer to behave as if everybody knows you. Then the people who *do* know you don't get any chances."

She wasn't satisfied. The sudden temper I had shown when I found her at the window had made her smell something.

"Bill, you are hiding something from me."

"No—honest, kid; why should I?"

"I don't know, Bill, but—did you get the papers?"

"Oh, I bought them, but I must have left them in the food shop."

"Didn't you read them?"

"Just glanced at them."

"What did they say?"

"They just had a little account of it—nothing much. Said you had disappeared."

"But, Bill—you said it was so important to read them carefully, to see what was happening, and now you say you only just glanced at them, and you haven't even brought them back. Bill—you *are* keeping something from me."

It was no good starting an argument. That would get her just as upset as the truth would. I sat down on the bed, and sat beside her, and took hold of her with my hands.

"I looked at them very carefully," I said. "There was a photo in them all."

"A photo? You mean a photo of *me?*"

I nodded. For a moment she looked completely bewildered. Then she suddenly remembered.

"It must have been the one Margery took—she's a girl at Benny's. She gave it to me, and I had forgotten all about it, but it must have been in my room somewhere."

"It's very like you," I said.

"But—that means they are absolutely certain to find me!" she said. "Bill, it means I can't go anywhere without being recognized. It means I have either to stay here in this room until someone finds me, or go and give myself up. It means there isn't a chance! It means they are certain to catch me! Bill—what can I do? What can I do?"

She was trembling now, and I thought she was going to cry. But she took hold of herself surprisingly.

"Is there any way out of this mess, Bill? Can you see any way out?"

I fondled her and looked into her eyes.

"I'll find a way. If it's the last thing I ever do, kid, I'm going to get you safely out of this."

"But what can you do, Bill? There's nothing you can do. You can't undo what has happened."

I shook my head. An idea was forming in my mind. It was crazy, and it was not clear yet, but was coming.

"You can't change what has happened," I said slowly, "but you can change some things."

I was speaking more to myself than to her, trying to sift that vague idea from the mass of things in my head, trying to harness a desperate plan that was growing clearer every second.

"What do you mean?" she asked.

"You can change some things," I said again.

"But what?"

I looked straight at her. The idea was hammering through my head now.

"People have changed," I said. "It wouldn't be the first time."

She took hold of my arms and shook me. "Bill—do stop saying things I can't understand. What is it you are going to do?"

"Give me time, kid," I said. "I must get it clearer and more settled before I can explain it. I've got a plan, but it needs some working out."

I was determined to keep it from her until I was ready to put it into action. No girl, not even the kid, would be able to stay home quietly if she knew exactly what was in my mind now.

"But I can't just stay here indefinitely, Bill," she said. "What is going to happen? Where shall I go next? Don't you realize how awful it is, sitting here hour after hour, not knowing what is going to happen?"

"I know," I said, "but I can't help it. I can't tell you just yet. I'm doing my best, and I've got a plan, and your part in it now is not to worry more than you can possibly help. There are one or two things I've got to do first, and then very soon we'll be out of here, and everything'll be all right."

"But what are these things you have to do first, Bill? Why don't you tell me what they are? Why won't you tell me what you mean by this plan of yours?"

"You must trust me, kid," I said earnestly. "I'm doing everything I can for the best."

"You're not going to do anything else wrong, are you, Bill? I'd rather give myself up, even knowing that it would drag you into it, than get into a life that means doing one wrong thing to cover up the first one, and then another to cover up the second. You're not doing anything else wrong, are you? Don't, Bill! Please don't!"

I smiled to reassure her.

"I'm only going to find out a few things, and make a few arrangements," I said.

"How long do you think I shall have to stay here?"

"Not long," I said. "Perhaps a week. But there's no real hurry. You're as safe here as anywhere at present."

"I wish you would tell me what you are thinking about," she complained.

"Don't ask me, don't hurry me, kid," I pleaded. "Please leave everything to me."

And then, looking down at her smooth, soft skin, and the face that I had always remembered so clearly ever since the first moment I saw her, I had to turn away. With her face right there in front of me, the whole idea was making me feel sick.

As far as I could see, it was her only chance. Before the sight of that photograph in the papers, when the possibility of that had not even come into my mind, then her chance seemed to lie in getting far enough away and living as a different person. But now, that was not enough. She would have to look a different person, too.

When the thought first came, it rushed through my head like a God-sent solution. Plenty of people had changed their faces. It was such a well-known thing that the subject had long been worn out as a music-hall joke. They were mostly old women, trying to look young again, but there did not seem to be any real reason why the same thing would not work for the kid. They said they could do almost anything with plastic surgery these days. All right. Let them try. Here was their chance to prove it. Here was a no-limit opportunity for them to make all the difference they could.

But now, walking through the streets in a hurrying effort to sort it all out clearly in my mind, every step was bringing a question. What about her? A girl with a face like the kid's—what would she say if you took it away from her? Something had stopped me from even mentioning the idea to her. It was not treating her like a person, like a human being. It sounded like turning her into a puppet thing, a parcel that you faked up so that you could smuggle it through the customs.

But if not—what else? We could not laugh off that photograph. She would never be safe. She could never be really safe anymore, as long as she had that face. She would have to see reason. She would have to realize that there was no other way out of it. She would have to grab this as the only chance there was. They could do it in a way that would make it not matter so very much to her. They could give her another nice one. That was their job, making nice ones.

Who was this "they"? Who was going to do all this? How was she going to get to them? Who was going to stop *them* from recognizing her? Who was going to make them agree to do it? Who was going to keep them quiet afterward?

The idea faded backward a bit, and started to look cockeyed. Why shouldn't a doctor do it? The world's greatest doctor—with a gun pressing into his back. A doctor and a nurse. A doctor and a dozen nurses—why shouldn't my kid have the very best attention in the world? God knows she deserves it! Yes—doctors and nurses and a smart, expensive nursing home, and machine guns all round the room to help them take an interest in the job and to keep their mouths shut. Like the gangsters. And afterward, when everything was all right, then bang! bang! bang! and everybody dead so nobody could tell.

I jerked myself up, shook off the haziness that was coming over me, pushed the play-acting picture out of my mind. Doctors were out of it. It would make her a million times safer in one way. But only in one way. Nothing was any good to her unless it led to freedom, real freedom, the kind of freedom when nobody talks because nobody *knows*.

My back was tickling again. They would do it for them, but not for her—was that the idea? They would do it for women whose only trouble was they were ugly old bags, but they wouldn't do it to get my kid out of this jam.

I dived into a bar, and swallowed a couple of drinks down quickly. What I had to do was keep my head, keep my back from tickling, keep my fists from bunching up so tight.

It would have to be a straight run, far enough away to leave that photograph behind. A straight run, using all the dark there was, praying to hell that nobody would spot her. She and I, with our heads down, butting right through the middle of everything. That was the only way.

I went out into the street again, and looked at the crowds of people passing along the pavements. Nobody was after them. They were safe. And so they were smug and righteous, too. There was not one of them who would not be eager to point to the kid, if they happened to see her and recognize her.

By the time I got back, after going round in rings for two or three hours, the kid was worse. She was very jumpy, and that night she cried for two hours without stopping.

"It won't be long now," I kept saying. "I'll soon have everything set."

"You keep saying that, Bill. You keep saying it won't be long. But you know it isn't true. You know it will go on forever. There's nothing we can do. There's nothing you or anyone else can do. It's just a question of waiting until they find me. What do you mean, it won't be long? You mean it won't be long before they find me!"

"I mean it won't be long before I get you right away into safety, kid. For God's sake believe that. I'll get you away from everyone, kid. It's the only thing that matters now. I'll do it all right. I swear it. I swear it to God!"

Chapter Twelve: "JUST TAKE ME AWAY"

"That's 'im!" said the lascar.

I followed his look across the smoky bar. "The short one?"

He nodded. "That's 'im. That's Cap'n Brand. I oughter know."

"You're absolutely sure about him?"

"'E done it afore. That's all I'm tellin' yer. 'E done it afore."

I pulled the pound note out of my pocket and chucked it on the bar.

"You'd better be right!" I told him.

He snapped the note up quickly.

"Yer swear yer won't tell 'im I told yer, mister? Fer Gawd's sake don't tell 'im 'oo told yer!"

Only waiting to gulp down his drink, he was off up the stairs as fast as he could go. I watched the newcomer cross the room and sit down at a table. Then I elbowed my way through the crowd round the bar and strolled across to him.

"Captain Brand?"

He looked up.

"What's that to you?"

I sat down opposite to him.

"What'll you drink?" I asked him.

His eyelids drooped down as he looked at me. For several seconds he didn't answer. Then he shrugged his shoulders.

"Why not? The drinks are straight enough here. Make it rye."

I beckoned the server.

"Two ryes," I said. Then I faced across the table and said, "I'm talking business."

"Uh?"

"I hear you're sailing soon."

He pulled at his pipe.

"Maybe," he said. "What's that to you?"

I waited while the man put the drinks on the table and went away again. Then I looked at the skipper hard.

"I'm looking for a quiet crossing," I said. Without taking his eyes off mine, he lifted his glass.

"Here's to you—and all your friends," he sneered.

I didn't get it.

"My friends?"

He sucked his glass empty, put it down on the table, and laughed.

"Yes—your friends," he said. "They're always trying to put naughty ideas into an honest man's head." Suddenly his face and voice went hard. "Now beat it, son! Back to your own side of the street! Captain Brand don't have a second drink with noseys!"

I gaped at him for a second, and then I laughed out loud. This was the first time I had ever been taken for a cop.

"Me?" I said. "By God! You've got the smoke in your eyes!"

"Uh? Well, maybe it's better if it stays there."

I looked at him, trying to size him up. Somehow I felt pretty sure the lascar's lead had been a right one. The skipper had shown no surprise. Even his quick suspicion of me was a pointer.

I put my guard right down.

"I'm looking for a ride for two," I said. "With no trumpets and no questions. It's a get-out!"

He smiled.

"Only for two? Are you sure you wouldn't like an invitation for the whole bloody police force?"

I frowned. He'd got it right into his head, and it was going to take some shifting. I searched my mind for some way of pushing the sense into him. Talking wouldn't do it. I tightened myself. So near to it, and now this fool idea of his was getting in the way. My back started tickling.

"Listen," I said suddenly. "If I can give you proof—will you talk it then?"

He shook his head.

"There's no proof," he said.

"No? Come with me and I'll show you."

"Come where?"

"In the bogs."

He gaped at me.

"What the hell are you getting at?"

"Come on and I'll show you proof all right," I said.

"You wouldn't be trying the funnies with Cap'n Brand, would you?"

"Come on," I said.

I stood up. He was bitten with guessing now. He got up and followed me across the bar and through the door and down into the lavatory.

There was nobody else there. As I went to take my jacket off, his hand went to his pocket as quick as a snake. I laughed at him.

"Hold it!" I said, tossing my jacket to him. Then I slipped my braces off my shoulders, and stood there facing him.

I spoke very quietly. "Just one little thing," I said slowly—"just one tiny little warning. No cracks. No laughs. No nothing. Don't forget."

And then I turned round quickly, and pulled up my shirt and bared my back to him.

"Does a cop wear those?" I asked.

I heard the breath whistle between his teeth, but that was all. I stuffed back my shirt, and pulled on my braces, and took my jacket from him.

"Let's talk," I said.

With a queer kind of look in his eyes he followed me back into the bar. As we got to the table he beckoned and ordered drinks.

"And when did you get the decorations?" he asked.

"You've seen them—that's enough," I told him. "Now let's talk."

He was ready enough to talk now. He could do it all right. There was nobody who could do it smoother than he could, he boasted.

"But you're asking me to risk a lot of trouble," he said.

"Nervous?"

He pushed his blue cap farther back on his head, so as to give me a better view of his scowl.

"Cap'n Brand's never been nervous of nothing!" he said fiercely.

"That's fine! Then let's get to details. How much do you want?"

"How much have you got?"

"A hundred's the top," I said.

"What? A hundred?" He faked up a big, deep chuckle. "You're fooling! What d'you take me for? What's a measly hundred quid for a cushy journey like I'll give you?"

"It's all there is."

"Nothing doing," he said.

I had seen the glitter in his eye. I stood up.

"It's all there is," I said.

"Here—wait a bit. No hurry, is there? Sit down and talk it over."

I sat down again, and he started wheedling. "You mean a hundred each, of course."

"I mean a hundred for the two."

"Well—let's say a hundred and fifty and call it a deal," he said.

"A hundred is all there is," I said impatiently. "Take it or leave it."

"All right. All right. But you're lucky. You won't find many men as obliging as Cap'n Brand! By the way—who's the other bloke?"

"It's a—it's my wife."

"Your—" He stopped with his glass halfway to his mouth. "A woman? You're running with a woman? You're barmy! It doubles your trouble and halves your chance." He paused, and his eyes went shiftier. Then he bent across the table and whispered, "Why don't you ditch her? I'll give you a hand."

My hands were under the table and I fought to keep them there. I could feel the blood coming up me, and my back was going mad. His face was swaying in front of my eyes. I bit my teeth together. He'd got to wait. He'd got to wait. The whole chance couldn't be smashed up now.

Just in time he must have seen it coming.

"All right! All right! It's your business! I don't want to butt in!"

I waited the best part of a minute before I spoke again.

"Where's the pickup?"

"I'll show you," he said. "Soon as we've had another drink. We'll be lying out, about three miles. My boy will be waiting with the launch, down at the wharf where I'll show you."

"Late Friday."

"Late Friday. The launch will wait for you. And you've got your end clear, haven't you? You won't forget anything, will you? That money's got to come up the ladder in front of you, see? And if it isn't there—all of it"—he rubbed a dirty hand over his face— "remember we'll be three miles out. You won't forget anything, will you?"

"You'll have it," I said.

He put his hand across the table.

"Shake on it, son. And there'll be flowers in the cabin. Cap'n Brand does everything in style. Ask anybody!"

I got up from my chair.

"Show me the wharf," I said.

As I sat in the train on the way back from the port, I felt that things were opening up. The skipper would be waiting. The launch would be there. There was too much greed in those shifty eyes for there to be any doubt about that. With a bit of luck in grabbing a car, we could do the whole thing in about three hours. The money would have to be Eggs's. "I've got nearly a hundred pounds saved," she had said. It would have to be that. If she loved the kid, she could never buy more than this with the money. It would have to be that. One of us on the run was quite enough. I couldn't risk landing myself in any new jam.

It was getting on for two in the morning by the time the train got me into town. I didn't want to go back to the room. Even going back to my room at this hour might help to draw someone's attention to the place. Idle curiosity, casual questions—those were things that in the ordinary way could be dealt with quickly and easily. But not now. As the time for escape came closer, no chance could be taken with anything. We might succeed, we might fail. But whichever way the ball was going to bounce, to give us the odds it was absolutely necessary that nobody's attention should be drawn to the room in any way at all. Just get people casually wondering, "Who's he? What's he do?" and that might be just enough to tip the scale.

I made my way to an all-night cafe, and sat there waiting for the time to pass, ordering coffee every now and then so that the waiters would not think I was using the place as a free shelter. All through the night, people were coming in and going out, and at first I was stiffening every time the door opened. But after the first half hour I got rid of the jumps, and passed the time reading newspapers that other people left behind.

As early as possible I was planning to get a bus out to the country, pay a quiet visit to Eggs, and get her to take her money out of the bank and give it to me. Then I could be back in plenty of time to get going at the right moment in the evening. I didn't want to go back to the kid before going out to Eggs. It would only mean just facing her again and leaving her again: And every time it was harder now. I could see her as she was at this very minute back in my room. If she was not asleep, she was lying like someone in a trance. Cowed and frightened. Waiting. Waiting. Waiting for nothing. With hardly the heart to listen to a lunatic who kept mumbling that everything would be all right.

"Don't worry, kid. Everything will be all right soon. It won't be long now."

It sounded flatter every time. It was starting to sound like a parrot talking. I didn't want to have to face her again until we were really ready to start. "Don't worry, everything will be all right." It wasn't cutting the ice with her any longer. Poor kid, how the hell could it? God! can't you think of something new to say to her? You gibbering slob, you got her into this, didn't you? Then get her out, and do it quick! What will happen if she goes off her nut with it all? What will happen if they find her? What will happen to you then? What will you say then, what will you do then, you god-blamed fool?

Oh, hell! I'm sorry! What's that? What's that? Who the hell cares about sorry? Let's see something happen. It's up to you. It won't be long now, eh? All right, it's up to you. Everyone is waiting. The whole damned place is waiting. Get her out of it quick, you mug, or you'll never shut your eyes in sleep again.

I wiped the damp off my forehead, paid the bill, and came out of the café to look for a bus. "It won't be long now." That was true this time. It wouldn't be long now.

"Hullo, kid!"
She was backed against the wall at the far side of the room, her eyes staring, facing the door as if she thought some horror was coming through it.
"It's me," I said.
Her head nodded slowly. Gradually, horribly gradually, the look of recognition came into her eyes. I locked the door and went over to her.
"Okay, kid?"
A hand came up and gripped my arm, then loosened, then gripped again, as if to make sure I was really there.
"Kid!"
Her lips moved. Her voice was so tiny I could only just hear it.
"I thought something had happened. I thought you were never coming."
Her guts were going. God help her, if it wasn't enough to make any girl's guts go. I put my arm round her, and held her tight and tried to stiffen her.
"It's all right, kid. Sorry I was so long."
Still the same tiny, lifeless voice.
"I thought you were never coming."
I forced a laugh. It went echoing round the room and came gibbering back.
"I couldn't help it, kid. I was busy. But everything's going to be all right now. Everything's fixed, and we start tonight. You been all right?"
She didn't answer. She just looked. I put my mouth down onto hers, but it didn't answer.
"Kid, everything's going to be all right. I've got everything fixed at last!"
Her lips trembled.
"When are they coming?" she asked.
"When are who coming?"
"When are they coming for me? The police. When are the police coming to arrest me?"
"They're not. Everything's going to be all right. I've got it all fixed."
She shook her head slowly.
"No, Bill. They're coming. They *are* coming. I can hear them coming. I can feel them coming. They've been coming all the time."
I shook her. "Get hold of yourself, kid. You've got to get hold of

yourself!"

She was in bad shape, and I wished I had not stayed away so long. She was in no kind of form to face up to things. Now, more than ever, she wanted her guts, and they had dodged her.

"I'm going to make some tea," I said. "Have some?"

She did not answer. She just stood where she was. I went over, and led her across to the chair and pushed her down into a sitting position. Then I lighted the gas ring and put the kettle on.

"Have a cigarette?" I asked.

She shook her head. But I shoved the thing into her mouth and held a match for it.

"Puff!" I told her.

She puffed and got it alight. I lighted one myself, and sat down facing her, waiting for the kettle to boil.

"It's just started to rain," I said. "You can hear it. Listen! It's coming down cats and dogs."

She nodded. She was looking straight in front of her.

"They need rain," I said. "They need it pretty badly. A chap was telling me how badly they need rain. The ground's getting hard as a rock."

She nodded.

"Well, they're getting it now, all right," I said. "Hark! Just listen to it coming down. They're getting it now all right, aren't they?"

She nodded.

"Isn't it funny," I said, "how there's always some people who want rain and some people who don't. You can't please everybody. Even the weather can't please everybody, can it?"

She nodded.

"No, it can't!" I rapped it out, making her jump.

"I—what did you say?"

"For God's sake, kid—try to snap out of yourself. Just try to loosen up your mind a bit. You're all pressed up tight. Just think about something else, if you possibly can. Talk about any damned thing— just for the sake of getting your mind eased off a bit."

She took a drag on her cigarette, and shifted herself on the chair.

"I can't understand you, Bill. You don't seem to be worrying anymore."

I took hold of both her hands in mine, and forced her to look straight at me.

"You don't believe that, kid," I said slowly. "You don't believe I'm not worrying. You know I am. Not in your way, but in mine. You know I've only got one thing inside my head, and that's you, and getting you safely away. You do know that, don't you?"

I felt a warm feeling wrap around me, as I thought I saw some of the trust and belief coming back into her eyes. But it was only a fleeting glimpse of her. The life in her eyes soon flickered and dimmed again.

"Bill," she said dully, "we'll have to face it. We can't just go on waiting here. I may as well give myself up and have done with it. It will have to come to that in the end, so it might as well be now. I think I'll be glad. Anything will be better than waiting here like this, knowing that it has got to come in the end. If I wait here much longer, I think it will send me mad."

"No!" I said quickly. "You don't have to wait here any longer. I've got everything fixed up and arranged. We are going right away, where nobody will ever know anything about it. You and me, right away to start living all over again, where nobody will ever know anything about us, nobody will look for us, nobody will matter to either of us, except you to me and me to you. That's where we're going, kid, and we're starting tonight!"

She looked straight at me, and answered very slowly and deliberately:

"I'm tired of hearing you say that, Bill. It doesn't mean anything, and you know it. You only keep saying it to try to cheer me up, and it doesn't cheer me up any longer. There is nothing you, or I, or anyone else can do about it. You know that, just as well as I do."

On the last few words her voice went fierce and trembling. She was fighting to keep control of herself, but she was nearly cracking.

"That isn't true!" I said, desperately trying to sound confident and calm. "I tell you that I've got everything completely mapped out. You haven't got to wait anymore. It's all ready. Everything is ready to start. We start now. Tonight!"

But it just wasn't getting inside her head at all. She was quivering now, and her eyes were blank and meaningless. She was no good to me like this. I needed all the best of her. She might have to help, and at any rate she'd got to keep her head clear.

With my left hand gripping her arm, I slapped my right palm hard across her cheek.

"Bill, what are you—!"

"Kid," I said, "for God's sake get this straight into your head. We are up against it. There is a way out, all completely fixed up. There won't be any slips if we go with our eyes open, but you've got to be keyed up for it. If you think you're going to trip up, then you *will* trip up. You've got to trust me. I can get you away, right clear away and safe forever, but only if you are ready to come. Now pull yourself together and hear what the plan is."

The flush died slowly away from her cheek. A bit of the something came back into her eyes. It had been just enough. It was almost the old kid looking at me now.

"Tell me," she said steadily.

The kettle was boiling. I got up and tipped some of the water into the teapot, and then poured out a couple of cups and handed one to her.

"Drink this," I told her; "it's just what you need. And now try to listen carefully."

Briefly, making it sound as nice and comfy as I could, I told her about the plans I had made down at the port.

"Can we trust him?"

"Yes," I said. "He wants the money. He'll be all right."

"But we haven't got the money."

"Yes, we have," I said. "Eggs had it saved up. I have been out there again, and she got it from the bank and gave it to me."

"But I still don't see how we are going to get down to the boat without someone recognizing me."

"It's dark and it's raining," I said, "and we'll be in a car all the way. No one will see you tonight."

"Auntie's car?"

"No. I daren't touch that. The police are already trying to trace you through your aunt. We'll take another one."

"You mean—steal one?"

"Borrow one," I said. "Three streets away from here there is a big cinema with a car park behind. I've sniffed it all out. The car park is dark. At eleven o'clock the people all come out. The park is crowded with people getting their cars. But half an hour before that there is just an odd person trickling out occasionally. It's about ten now. In half an hour, with your face muffled up, we walk along and duck down into that car park and hide between the cars. Then we wait for one of the car owners to come out."

"But—I don't understand. Why do we wait for the owner?"

With my hands I took hold of her shoulders and held them tight.

"Now, listen, kid," I said. "You've got to remember that we are running away for our lives. If any little thing happens, you've just got to remember that it's nap or nothing for us. If I have to knock someone out, I won't be really hurting him. I'll just be keeping him quiet while we are getting away. Understand?"

She shook her head. "I still don't see why you want to wait for the owner of the car."

"Because we can't add to the risks that we've got to run," I said. "If we just take a car, and the owner misses it and reports it to the police, then the cops may be looking for the car, and they might pick us up on the way to the port. But if we take the owner with us, he won't be able to tell anybody anything."

"But you don't mean you are going to—" she hesitated, not wanting to say it.

I shook my head and smiled. "Nothing, kid," I said. "Absolutely nothing. I may just have to keep him quiet; but it's just like boxing—nothing to worry about, I promise."

She looked steadily into my eyes. "I leave it all to you, Bill," she said slowly. "Without you I just wouldn't know what to do at all. Just take me away, Bill. That's all I want."

I put my arm round her and held her close for a minute. "We're on, our way," I said.

Chapter Thirteen: FLIGHT

We crept down the stairs and out into the street. The heavy rain was over, but it was still a nasty, drizzling night, and there was practically no one about. With her face well hidden, we set off in the direction of the cinema.

"Whatever happens, don't get far away from me," I said. "And do exactly what I tell you."

The cinema was on a corner, and the car park was round the back, right away from the cinema entrance. You could get to the park from both directions, but it might have aroused suspicion if we had entered the park without approaching from the direction of the cinema. We had to risk passing the full glare of the entrance.

"Snuggle your face right down, as if you're hiding from the rain," I whispered.

We hurried past, and rounded the corner and came to the park. We walked in, heading down the clear space between the two closely packed lines of cars.

"Which is yours, sir?"

The voice pulled me up with a jump. I had forgotten that there might be a carpark attendant.

"Duck in there between those two," I whispered to her, and pointed. She walked quickly between the two cars.

"Have you got your ticket, sir?"

I fumbled in my pocket, edging away a little so as to put the barrier of a car between me and the kid.

"Here it is," I said.

As he moved toward me, clicking on his torch, I clipped him clean and caught him as he sagged. Then I lugged him through between the cars as quickly as I could, and laid him on the ground behind them. It had hardly made a sound, and I didn't think the kid had even seen. But it had cut our time limit down, because I didn't know how long he would take to come round.

I went back to her.

"All right?" I whispered.

"Yes," she said steadily, trying to cover up the excitement and anxiety in her voice. She was in good shape now.

In the darkness, crouched there between the cars, I put my arm around her and held her tight.

"We shan't be long now, kid," I said. "Just keep the way you are.

Just keep cool and quiet, and remember there's nothing to worry about."

We waited there, while the seconds dragged by. If nobody came soon, I'd have to see to the attendant again. Or if all the people came out in pairs—

The sound of footsteps was coming from the entrance to the park. I could see him silhouetted against the street light. By a stroke of luck the very first one was a man alone.

"Keep well down so that he doesn't see your head," I whispered.

He walked across to a car the other side of the park. I heard him fumbling with his keys. As he opened the door and slipped into the seat, I grabbed the kid and rushed her across the space between. We got there just before he closed the door.

"We want a lift," I said.

"I beg your pardon?"

Sitting there, straining his head out of the door trying to see me, his jaw was just right for it. Giving him all I'd got, to keep him quiet for as long as possible, I shoveled him across onto the other front seat. Then I put my hand inside and undid the catch of the back door.

"You get in the back," I told her. "I'll keep him beside me, so that I can keep my eye on him."

His keys were dangling from the dashboard. I got into the driving-seat, turned on the engine, and pressed the starter. The engine coughed once, and then got going. Inside of a minute we were out of the park and heading down the road.

"Keep yourself well down away from the windows," I said over my shoulder.

I fumbled to find the instrument light, and clicked it on for a second to see the petrol. The gauge said three-quarters full. Plenty for the time being.

I glanced at the man by the side of me. He was slumped there with his head on his chest. Anyone happening to see him by the street lights would only think he was asleep.

"We're as good as there, kid," I said, with a feeling of triumph mounting in me.

It was a decent car, with a nice turn of speed, and I pushed her along as fast as I dared on the wet roads. So far everything was going perfectly to plan. If only the luck would hold, we had got practically nothing to fear now. Within three hours we should be on the wharf, getting into the launch, climbing up the ladder, shaking ourselves clear and free from everything,

We were nearly clear of the town by the time the man beside me stirred. I heard a tiny sound in the back of the car. I felt her eyes on me. With her in the back, there was nothing to do but just give him the same clean thing again.

I could not risk stopping yet. Holding the wheel with my left hand, I measured it up carefully, and suddenly swiveled in my seat and brought my right arm across at him. He sagged down again, but in the sudden lunge I had jerked the wheel badly over. There was a scream from the back of the car as we shot across the road in a slithering skid. I caught a glimpse of a cyclist wobbling in front of me as I fought with the wheel. Just as the car straightened up again, I felt the jar of hitting him.

"Bill, you—you've knocked him over."

Gripping the wheel, I drove straight on without slackening speed.

"We can't wait. Someone will see to him. Keep your face away from the window."

I snatched a glance round, and saw that she was kneeling on the seat looking out of the back.

"Keep your face away from that window!" I shouted.

"But, Bill—that car that was standing by the side of the road there—I believe it is coming after us."

"Nonsense!" I said; "for God's sake keep your face away from the window."

But in the driving-mirror I could see the lights of the car she was referring to. It must have been about two hundred yards behind. It might have seen us knock the cyclist over. It might be following us. I put my foot down harder. We could shake it off.

I threw the car fiercely round the next few bends in an effort to draw clear. But still, every time there was a straight piece of road those same lights were in the driving-mirror. They seemed to be gaining on us. Then suddenly, faint but unmistakable came the dingling clang of a police car gong.

I set my teeth and stiffened. Of all the impossible bits of luck, I had knocked that cyclist over in sight of a police car.

"Keep your head down out of sight," I said again.

I had picked a good car. The needle went 55, 60, 65, as we tore through the straggles of the suburbs and headed along the main road. But still those lights kept coming in the mirror. And still, every minute or two, I could hear that dingling clang, if anything nearer now.

As we flashed around the wet bends, I glanced at the man beside me. If I got well over to the right-hand side of the road, opened the door, and pushed him out so that he fell into the middle, that might stop them.

Edging the car across the road, I leaned across the slumping body beside me and felt for the door-catch. But just as I found it I changed my mind. That wouldn't be any good. That would be only fixing things up for certain. They would have my number, and if I dropped a body out of the car they would put in the kind of call that would have me picked up anywhere in half an hour.

Fighting my mind for an answer, I drove on and on, hardly slowing for the corners, taking all the chances with what little traffic there was. But still those lights in the mirror came nearer, nearer. A hundred yards. Fifty yards. Hardly anything now.

"Don't lose your head, kid," I said. "Get ready to jump out and run when I tell you."

They were creeping up. The clang of the gong was right on top of us now. I swerved once or twice to keep them back, but the road was wide and they kept creeping up. The needle said just on seventy now, and it wouldn't do another inch. Out of the corner of my eye I saw the nose of the other car level with my back wheels. For a moment I felt almost paralyzed by a blinding, thwarted fury. As it crept on, halfway beside me now, I wrenched the wheel hard over. There was the bang of a tire, the crash of tearing metal, and a scream. And then the whole road seemed to shake and shudder, and things went upside down and we were flung through the darkness.

In the sudden silence I sat there slightly dazed for a few seconds. Dimly a pain was tearing at my hands, but I fought it back. Suddenly, clear and cold, as if I were an onlooker, I sorted out the scene. The car was right way up again now. It must have turned clean over as we had gone down the bit of embankment from the road. The other car was about ten yards away. I could see, by the way its lights were, that it was on its side. No sound came from it at all. The only sound from anywhere was a whimpering little moan from the kid.

I tried to open the door, but it had jammed. Reaching upward, I managed to force back the sliding roof. The man beside me was quiet and still. I strained in the darkness. It looked like blood on his face. I scrambled out through the roof and tried the back door of the car. It came open, and the kid, leaning against it, flopped out onto the running board.

"How bad are you, kid?"

She tried to stand up, but she swayed and flopped back onto the running board, moaning. At least she could moan. There was still no sound from the other car.

There was no time to be lost. We weren't stopped yet. As long as I was on my feet, we weren't stopped yet. I took her up in my arms and carried her a few yards away from the car, and laid her gently down on the grass. Then I went quickly back to the car.

We still had a chance. The launch was waiting. The ladder was there. This car wasn't ours. This man was a stranger to us, just giving us a lift. The cyclist was nothing to do with us, because I hadn't been driving. This smash was nothing to do with us, because he had been driving. We were just strangers, getting a lift. I couldn't tell if or how soon the cops would crawl out of that other car. Someone else would come along, anyway. If this fellow looked like the driver, then they would not be hunting for us.

Standing on the bonnet of the car and reaching over through the roof, I lugged him across into the driving-seat and pushed one of his arms down through the spokes of the steering wheel. He was the driver, clear enough now. Unless he woke up and talked.

He might be dead already. It wasn't for me. It was for her. I didn't need it. I could get out all right, but it still kept her chance going.

He was probably dead already. As he slumped there with his arm through the wheel, I put my hand down and took hold of him by the back of the neck, and with a quick lunging thrust I brought his forehead crunching down on the base of the windscreen.

Then, carrying her in my arms, I struggled up the grass side of the embankment back to the road.

"Bill!"

She could speak. She was going to be all right. I knew she was going to be all right. It couldn't be anything much. It couldn't end like this. Not anyone, anything, could hurt her while I had her.

I started to carry her along the road. The launch was there. The ladder was there. Everything was waiting. Nothing could stop us now.

"We're nearly there, kid," I said to her. "We mustn't stop now. We're nearly there."

Behind me, the lights of a car came searching through the darkness. I carried her into the middle of the road, and stood there to stop the car. It slowed, hesitated, came again. But I stood there right in the middle of the road and it had to stop.

The driver opened the door and came running out.

"We want a lift," I told him.

"Good God!" he said. "Quick. I'll take you to the hospital."

"To hell with the hospital!" I said. "Get in and drive us. I'll tell you where to go."

And then, suddenly, in the glare of his headlights I got a look at her. Her face was red and shiny, and her mouth was strained open.

I looked again. Not like this we couldn't go on. There was just time for a quick pause to get her seen to first. The launch would wait. We'd got time for that.

"Take us to the hospital!" I said.

He opened the back of the car and I carried her in.

"Do you know where the nearest one is?"

"Yes, I live in the next town," he said.

"Then get a move on, can't you?"

As we drove along, I held her close to me, felt the warmth of her, held her closer, closer.

He pulled up outside the hospital, and jumped out and opened the door of the car.

"Let me give you a hand," he said.

I lifted my foot and kicked him away.

"Keep your hands off her," I told him.

I carried her up the steps and through the entrance and into the hall. White-coated people were coming swiftly at me.

"In here. Lay her down on this table."

"I'm not leaving go of her," I said. "Bring your best doctor, quick. Your best one. Tell him if he doesn't come quick I'll—"

"Lay her down on this table. Here—let me take her."

I tugged her tighter to me.

"Nobody's taking her!" I shouted. "She belongs to me! She's mine! Mine! Nobody's taking her!"

But they took her just in time. And just in time one of them put an arm round my waist, as the pain came tearing up my arms and the room went muzzy and gray.

Chapter Fourteen: THE DREAM

The heat of the day had passed, but the sun was still warm. In the shade of the trees on the top of the ridge it was never too hot. But now the shade had moved round, and the sun, falling full on the side of my face for the first time, was doing its best to wake me up. I rolled over on the soft grass, rubbing my eyes and yawning.

The dream had been there again. The dream was often there when I was sleeping up on the ridge. From under the trees you could see the country rolling and tumbling for miles away to the westward, and it must be very nearly time for the incredibly ancient Ford to come rattling up the track below the ridge. That was when the dream came, up on the ridge there, waiting for the Ford to bring her back.

It was not always quite the same. Sometimes one part would be vividly clear while another part would be vague and elusive. Sometimes it would all be reversed. Sometimes the order would get so jumbled up that it would hardly make sense at all. But the same things were always there, in this dream that was really a memory.

It started with blood. Sometimes, if the dream was going particularly badly, the blood would come at the end, and stay for ages. But usually it started with blood. Blood that was over my hands and everything else. Blood that would not stop. Blood that was coming from nowhere, from everywhere, and would not stop coming. It was precious blood, too. Not just ordinary blood, but specially valuable blood, so that all the time it was coming, and would not stop, I was losing something. It was not my blood, and yet all the time it was coming I was losing, losing, losing.

And the blood had eyes. Somehow or other it had eyes, and wherever it went it looked at me, and wherever I looked, there it was, red and wet and looking at me with eyes. I had seen those eyes before, but the dream would not tell me where. The dream always pretended that they were just the blood's eyes, and I always had to wait until I had waked up before I could remember whose they were and where I had seen them before. And of course, although I knew that I had seen them before, they were very different now that they were the blood's eyes. They were no longer soft and warm the way they had been when I had known them before. They were hard and cold and frightened now, so frightened that I wanted to say kind and reassuring things to them. But I could not, because every time I tried to speak to them they sank backward, and the blood gulfed over them, hiding them until I stopped trying to speak to them.

And sometimes, every now and then, the blood would part, like water running away from a greasy surface, and a face would come peeping through it. The odd thing was that the face had nothing whatever to do with the eyes. The eyes were the blood's eyes, and I had seen them before, often, long before the dream started, even if they were quite different now. But the face was nothing to do with them. It was a new face, completely strange. I was sure I had never seen *that* before the dream. And as far as I had been able to make out, nobody at all had ever seen it before the dream, because the dream had invented it. The face never existed before the dream started, although the eyes had been around for a long time before. But then, the face was nothing to do with the eyes.

Suddenly, just as I was beginning to think that everything was always going to be blood, it went dark. Everything went dark. I searched everywhere for a light, but everywhere was dark. For days and days it went on being dark everywhere, without a glimmer of a light at all. And gradually I realized that it was not really dark everywhere, but only dark where I was. The reason why I had not been able to find any light was because I had been instinctively looking for the dark all the time. And as soon as I found some light—which was quite by accident, because I was looking for the dark—it scared me so much that I went scuttling back to a place that was darker than ever.

Sometimes this hiding and skulking in the dark went on for the rest of the dream. But usually the darkness in the dream broke suddenly, and I was standing, fidgeting restlessly, in a small, bare room. One of my arms was hung in a sling, the other hand thick with bandages. Presently the door opened and a woman came in.

"You can see her now," she said.

"It's about time!" I said, moving quickly toward the door.

"Just a minute, please." She put her arm out to stop me. "Before you go in, I want to warn you."

"What do you mean?" I said. "They told me she was all right. They told me there was no danger. They told me she could come out straight away."

"So she can," the matron said. "It is quite true that there is no danger. The injuries are only superficial. Given ordinary care, there is no reason for anxiety. But I want to warn you before you see her that—" She hesitated.

"What are you getting at?"

"I have never seen her before, of course," she said, "but her face has suffered considerably. It is just possible that you won't instantly, er—recognize—"

Limp and cold I stood there, as her words faded away from me. I closed my eyes and saw the only face in the world, with the gay little uptilted nose and the mouth that was always just going to smile. Was it gone? Had I taken that away from her?

And then the other side of it came banging into my mind. Did it mean that the photograph in the papers was no longer a photograph of her? Did it mean that we could come out of the darkness? Did it mean—

"Don't you *want* to see her?" The matron was speaking again, impatiently now.

I pulled myself back to it.

"Give her to me!" I said.

She turned, and I followed her up some stairs and along a passage and into a sickly smelling room.

Then, sleepy with sleep, and tired with the dreaming, I thought I saw the flutter of a handkerchief over the long mound that hid the track about a mile away. I stood up and cupped my hands to my mouth.

"Yoo-hoo!"

It went down the side of the ridge, echoing over the rise and fall of the ground, and with my eyes more wide-awake now, I could see the quick double wave of the handkerchief which showed that she had heard. I scrambled down the slope, coming to the vague track of rubbed-away grass that was the only road there was. From around the bend came the ancient Ford, steaming bravely.

It stopped just short of where I was standing. I ran forward and jumped onto the running board.

"Move over, lady!"

She slid across the seat, and I climbed in and took the wheel.

"Where to?" I asked.

"There's no place like it," she answered.

I let in the clutch and we chugged on up the slope. As we topped it, there in the distance was a little bungalow, sheltered by a belt of ragged trees.

She sighed contentedly.

"Still there!" she said. "Every time I leave it, I'm half afraid that when I get back I'll find it really isn't true after all. But it's still there."

I took one hand off the wheel and rested it round her shoulders.

"Good day?" I asked her.

She nodded.

"Hot and tiring," she said, "but good all the same. I bought lots of things, and spent all your money. Oh!—" She broke off excitedly, and dived down with her hand to get something out of her basket. "I didn't tell you the big news. A letter!"

"Who from?"

"From England. Guess!"

"From England?" A sudden fear went shooting through me, a sudden fear that everything had failed. "From England? Then somebody knows! Somebody knows where—"

She laughed.

"Silly Bill! Where's your memory? I told you weeks ago that I had written to Aunt Ethel. It's from her."

"Eggs?" I laughed with sudden relief. "Good old Eggs! What does she say?"

"It's a lovely long letter. You must read it when we get back. She says her new man is not nearly as efficient as you were, and of course not half as handsome. She says"—she hesitated, and then said very quietly—"she says the police have at last stopped asking her questions."

I tightened my hand on her shoulder. I knew there was nothing that I could say that she would not be thinking, too. It was months in the past, all of that. It was thousands of miles away. But how long it would stay that far away, we sometimes did not dare to wonder. Here, we had told ourselves a million times, there was no way of anyone knowing. Here, we were different people, living a different life. Here, everything was easier, cleaner, fresher. Here, your past was your affair. Nobody asked. Here, you had a chance. But for how long—

At last they had stopped asking her questions.

We drove on in silence to the bungalow.

Gathering up an armful of parcels from the back seat of the car, I staggered up the three wooden steps in front of the bungalow, pushed the door open with my knee, and tipped them onto the table that stood in the center of the big main room. She followed close behind, adding some more to the pile. I stood back and surveyed them.

"Looks as if you've been buying up the whole town, kid!"

She laughed.

"I have, Bill. I've been shamefully and marvelously extravagant. I just bought and bought and bought. I began to think that I'd got up such a momentum of buying that I wouldn't ever be able to stop. It was grand! Of course, I may as well tell you straight away that you are pretty well ruined. We shall have to live on grass for the next few weeks. But they say the air here is very nourishing. Shall we put our heads out of the window and have our supper?"

She was busily unpacking the parcels as she talked. It was good to see her like that. It was good to hear the happiness bubbling out of her. I leaned back against the wall, and watched her moving quickly and eagerly about the room. Her body was young and lovely, just as lovely as ever it had been. As she busied herself, with her back to me, she was just the same as ever.

She finished unpacking the things she had bought and putting them away, and then turned round to me.

"Ready for something?" she asked.

I nodded.

"How about beans?"

"Beans would be fine," I said. "And coffee?"

"Beans and coffee for two coming up, sir!"

She lighted the oil stove and started opening a can.

"No news for *me?*" she demanded.

"Well, I'll be damned!" I exclaimed. "I was waiting there, itching to tell you, and then I forgot!"

"Well, out with it!"

"They've put up the pay at the ranch," I said.

She spun round and faced me.

"Yours, Bill?"

"Mine and two or three others, yes."

"How much?"

"Another four shillings."

She put down the can, bounded across the room, and threw her arms round me and hugged me.

"Oh, Bill," she said, "how rich we are! You must be doing marvelously. You must be working frightfully hard. Bill, aren't we lucky? Aren't we just the luckiest people in the world? We've got everything!"

She squeezed me with excitement. To have her like that was worth anything in the world.

"That's nothing, kid," I said. "Someday we'll have a whole ranch of our own. There's nothing that can stop you and me."

For a minute or two she stayed there, snuggling up against my shoulder. And then together we went back over to the stove to heat the beans.

Out with the dawn on the rolling earth it was good there. The sun came up gradually, and in three or four hours it would be hot; but then you would rest while the worst of it went, and until then the warmth and the long, stretching space were satisfying things. The working used your strength, but it never really tired you. It was hard, and it took out the restless force, but it never left you really tired. That was the air, the air and the rolling distance that went on and on as far as you could see. There was something about it that made the whole thing different. Everything fitted. You and the rest of everything fitted together, instead of being at war. It was like a world with a valve left open, a different world because it wasn't tight and shut and cramped. It was a world that looked forward, never back: a world that left you free.

Away to the left, beyond that faint hazy smudge in the distance, beyond the hills that you just could not see, and on down to the port, and then on and on across the sea, there was the other side of everything. Sometimes, but not very often, I thought back to all those things from which we had snatched ourselves. Sometimes, even here, I could feel for a moment the tenseness that had clamped itself around us there. The waiting, hiding in the dark. The touch and go of every minute, hour after hour. The pleading pain in her eyes. The listening for footsteps, the crouching in corners. The endless stumbling journey, perhaps to nowhere. The aching tiredness, the longing to go to sleep. But now it all seemed very far away. This, the life that was round us now, was climbing on top of the past. I unloosed the horse from the plow I had been driving, and slapped it on the buttock with the palm of my hand. It knew the way, and set off contentedly toward the sheds.

"Next time you are making a trip to the town, kid, will you try to remember to get me some razor blades?"

We were sitting outside the bungalow together in the soft evening air. She had just put down some sewing she was doing, because the light was beginning to fade.

She did not answer. Thinking that perhaps her mind was roaming and she had not heard, I asked her again. This time I knew she must have heard, but she still hesitated, and before she spoke she lowered her head, fixing her eyes on the ground.

"Why not ask one of the men to get them for you? There's always one of them going in, nearly every day. It would be better to do that if you need them badly, because I don't quite know when I'll be going in again."

She spoke awkwardly, almost as if she were embarrassed. And

when I tried to read her eyes, she deliberately turned her head to avoid me.

"I'm not in that hurry," I said. "I can easily wait till you go again."

"No, I should get someone else to get them for you," she pressed.

It was strange to hear her talking like that, because one of her greatest pleasures was driving the rickety old Ford into the town. She usually went at least once a fortnight, always making a day's outing of it, and spending the previous evening checking through her stores, and asking me what she could get from the shops for me.

"All right," I said. "If it's too much trouble for you to do it!"

She swung round immediately, putting a hand quickly on my arm.

"Oh, Bill! I didn't mean that. You know I wouldn't mean that! It's just that I don't quite know when I'll be going into town again. I may not go for ages."

"But you enjoy it so much, kid. What's the idea in knocking the visits off?"

"Oh, I don't know," she said vaguely. "It's so lovely here, it seems rather silly to go dashing off to a town unless it's absolutely necessary."

"Well—you please yourself, kid," I said. But I was puzzled. It was such a sudden change of attitude. And I was sure she had been awkward about saying it. It stuck in my mind, so that quite a while later I brought the subject up again.

"Kid—is there some special reason why you don't want to go into town again?"

"No, Bill. Not really," she said. But her voice was uncertain.

"I believe there is, kid. Tell me."

"No, there's nothing, Bill. It's only just my silliness. You wouldn't understand."

"What wouldn't I understand?"

She did not answer, and I noticed that again her head was turned deliberately away.

"What wouldn't I understand?" I asked again. "Did something happen the last time you were there? Do tell me, kid. I know there's something."

"No, really it wasn't anything, Bill." She was trying hard to sound unconcerned. "We are just making something out of nothing. It wasn't anything, really."

"Why not tell me?"

"You—you wouldn't understand, Bill. It's just silly of me. There was nothing, really. It was only a couple of kids. They didn't mean anything."

"Kids? What did they do? What happened?"

"They didn't do anything." Her face was still turned away, but it sounded as if she was crying.

"Do tell me what happened, kid," I urged her.

She waited for a minute. Then, as if speaking to herself, she said, "They were only children. They didn't mean it. They didn't understand."

"What did they do, kid?"

"They didn't do anything much. It was just something they said." It was clear she was crying now.

"Who were they? What did they say?"

"They were just two children in the street," she said in a tiny, distant voice. "They were playing as I came up to them. And then they looked up as I got near them, and"—her voice was wobbly—"and they pointed at me and started calling something out."

"What was it?"

She answered in such a tiny whisper that I could only just hear. "Funnyface," she said.

My hand was on her arm. But until she yelped I didn't know my nails were biting into her. She suddenly wriggled her arm away.

"You're hurting me," I heard her saying.

"Who said that?" I was almost talking to myself.

"Who said what?"

"What you just told me. Who said that to you?"

"It was only a couple of kids, Bill. I told you it was only that. It was nothing. It's only my silliness, really. I shouldn't have mentioned it."

"Nobody's going to say things like that," I said.

I felt her shaking me.

"Bill—they were only children. You mustn't start getting like that."

"Nobody's going to do that," I said.

"Bill—there's no need to get like that! Bill—*you're all tightened up, the way you used to get! Please—oh, please listen to me, Bill!*"

I pushed her hands away from me, and stood up. "Nobody's going to do it," I whispered.

But her arms came round my neck, and her eyes got right in the way of mine.

"Bill! Don't talk like that. Don't look like that. Bill—you put me in heaven. Please keep me there. Please! Please!"

The tears were still hanging around her eyes. I wiped the two wet beads off her cheekbones with the tip of my little finger. Then

I suddenly picked her off her feet, and carried her in my arms through the doorway into the bungalow. Softly, gently, I laid her on the bed.

"They don't know what they're talking about," I said. "You're lovely."

She smiled, and shook her head.

"Not anymore, Bill."

"Yes. More than ever. More than anyone."

"Bill! You're squeezing me so I can't breathe!"

"I love you," I said.

"That's what matters, Bill. That's all that matters. Never think about anything else at all. Just keep on saying that. Keep saying it and saying it."

"I love you. I love you. I'll smash the guts out of anyone who looks at you!"

THE END

FILM NOIR CLASSICS

THE PITFALL Jay Dratler
"Dratler's novel is darker, sleazier and less forgiving than the film it inspired. A brutal portrait of blind lust and self-destruction... a stellar example of 1940s American noir." —Cullen Gallagher, *Pulp Serenade.* Filmed in 1948 with Dick Powell, Lizabeth Scott, Jane Wyatt and Raymond Burr.

FALLEN ANGEL Marty Holland
"This story, about a small-time grifter who lands in a central California town and hooks up with a femme fatale, is straight out of the James M. Cain playbook."—Bill Ott, *Booklist.* Filmed in 1945 with Dana Andrews, Alice Faye and Linda Darnell.

THE VELVET FLEECE
Lois Eby & John C. Fleming
"We guarantee your head will be spinning with double-crosses and you'll be talking out of both sides of your mouth before you finish...."
—*Evening Star.* Filmed as *Larceny* in 1948 starring John Payne, Joan Caulfield and Dan Duryea.

SUDDEN FEAR Edna Sherry
"This is a thoroughly exciting read, with brilliant pacing, which makes you absolutely desperate to know how everything will pan out."
—Kate Jackson. Filmed in 1952 with Joan Crawford, Jack Palance and Gloria Grahame.

HOLLOW TRIUMPH Murray Forbes
"...a disturbed personality done in the noir tradition... an atmospheric and evocative yarn that spans the late 30s to through WWII."—Amazon reader. Filmed in 1948 with Paul Henreid and Joan Bennett as *The Scar.*

THE DARK CORNER /
SLEEP, MY LOVE Leo Rosten
"The slang is tangy, the plots magnetic, the suspense sweet, the hilarity edgy... For all lovers of vintage noir."
—Donna Seaman, *Booklist.* Filmed in 1946 and 1948 with Lucille Ball, Clifton Well, Claudette Colbert and Robert Cummings.

DEADLIER THAN THE MALE
James Gunn
"The attitude of the book... reels between black comedy and surrealism drenched in a misanthropy that is occasionally stunning."—Ed Gorman. Filmed as *Born to Kill* in 1947 with Lawrence Tierney and Claire Trevor.

9 798886 010886